The Octavian Cases

Volume 17 of

The Casebooks

Of Octavius Bear

Harry DeMaio

"Alternative Universe Mysteries for Adult

Animal Lovers"

Paperback ISBN 978-1-78705-989-4
ePub ISBN 978-1-78705-990-0
PDF ISBN 978-1-78705-991-7

Published by MX Publishing
335 Princess Park Manor, Royal Drive,
London, N11 3GX
www.mxpublishing.com

Cover layout and construction by
Brian Belanger

THE CASEBOOKS OF OCTAVIUS BEAR

Dedicated to GTP

A Most Extraordinary Bear

And to the late Ms. Woof

An Extremely Sweet and Loving

Dog

Acknowledgements

These books have evolved over a long period of time and under a wide range of influences and circumstances. I am indebted to many people for helping to bring Octavius and his cohorts to the printed and electronic page. Thanks most especially to my wife, Virginia, for her insights and clever suggestions as well as her unfailing enthusiasm for the project and patience with its author.

To my sons, Mark and Andrew and their spouses, Cynthia and Lorraine, for helping to make these tomes more readable and audience friendly. To Cathy Hartnett, cheerleader-extraordinaire for her eagerness to see this alternate universe take form. To Jack Magan, Paul Bernish, David Chamberlain, Dan Walker, Dan Andriacco, Amy Thomas, Luke Benjamin Kuhns, Derrick Belanger, Gretchen Altabef and Zohreh Zand for their enthusiastic encouragement. And to all of my generous Kickstarter backers.

Kudos to Jim Effler, the late Bob Gibson and Brian Belanger for their wonderful illustrations and covers. Thanks, of course, to Sharon, Steve and Timi Emecz at MX Publishing for giving The Great Bear and his gang of Octavians a wonderful home.

If, in spite of all this support, some errors or inconsistencies have crept through, the buck stops here. Needless to say, all of the characters, situations, and narratives are fictional. Some locations, devices, historical figures and events are real.

Thanks to Wikipedia for providing facts and figures used throughout this book.

Also by Harry DeMaio

The Octavius Bear Series – Books 1-16

Note to the Reader:

The Casebooks of Octavius Bear are designed to be read individually, independently and in any order. That is why some preliminary information is repeated in each volume.

This book is no exception. However, you may get a fuller understanding of some of the dynamics and characters in this Volume 17 if you have already read Volume 13 through 16. Not necessary, mind you. Just a suggestion.

In any event, I hope you enjoy this story. Thanks for taking it up.

The Development of Civilization Volume 17
Part 1
<u>Our Origins</u>

From "An Introduction to Faunapology"

by Octavius Bear Ph.D.

About 100,000 years ago, according to scientific experts, a colossal solar flare blasted out from our Sun, creating gigantic magnetic storms here on Earth. These highly charged electrical tempests caused startling physical and psychological imbalances in the then population of our world. The complete nervous systems of some species were totally destroyed. For example, "Homo Sapiens" lost all mental and motor capabilities and rapidly became extinct. Less developed species exposed to the radiation were affected differently. Four-footed and finned mammals, birds and reptiles suddenly found themselves capable of complex thought, enhanced emotions, self-awareness, social consciousness and the ability to communicate, sometimes orally, sometimes telepathically, often both. Both speech production and speech perception slowly progressed with the evolution of tongues, lips, vocal cords and enhanced ear to brain connections. Many species developed opposable digits, fingers or claws, further accelerating civilized progress. Some others (most fish and underground dwellers) were shielded from radiation and remained only as sentient as they were before the blast. This event is referred to as The Big Shock. It remains under intensive study.

Positive in our knowledge that we are not alone in the cosmos, my staff and I are heavily engaged in Project Multiverse, successful searches for alternate universes, especially those in which "Homo Sapiens" continues to live and hopefully, prospers. This book touches on some of the results of that project.

The Players

- **Octavius Bear** – Mega-sized Kodiak; Narcoleptic war hero; Consulting Detective; Scientist; Inventor; Seeker of Justice; Gazillionaire CEO and owner of Universal Ursine Industries; Gourmet/Gourmand; Bee Keeper; Somewhat sedentary and grouchy just on general principles.
- **Mauritius (Maury) Meerkat** – Narrator; Assistant to Octavius; Theatrical Agent; African *émigré* with a French-Dutch background; clever with a shady history.
- **Bearoness Belinda Béarnaise Bruin Bear** *(nee Black)* – Gorgeous polar superstar with the Aquashow, ***"Some Like It Cold;"*** Wife of Octavius; Extremely rich widow living part time in Polar Paradise in the Shetlands; Owner-pilot of the last flying Concorde SST.
- **Arabella Bear** – Hybrid bear cub prodigy; Twin daughter of Bearoness Belinda and Octavius. Now a juvenile.
- **McTavish Bear** – Hybrid bear cub prodigy; Twin son of Bearoness Belinda and Octavius. Now a juvenile.
- **Mlle Giselle Woof** – Bichon Frisé – Former Governess to the Twins. Now on her way to becoming a Tarot Specialist and actress.
- **Frau Ilse Schuylkill** – Octavius' beautiful Swiss she-wolf estate manager/cook/pilot/security officer with many other mysterious and military talents. She rescued Octavius from his dive off the Breakurbach Falls while he was struggling with his nemesis, Imperius Drake.
- **Wyatt Where** – The Colonel – Another wolf; Former military intelligence officer who had retired to a security post at the Bank of Lake Michigan in Chicago and then quit to join Octavius; The Frau's Mate.
- **Howard Watt** – Porcupine; High tech security authority who also left the Bank to join Octavius; Alternate Universe specialist; Quantum Mechanics, laser and particle beam accelerator expert.
- **Marlin** – Dolphin (sic) – the Prince of Whales' one-time Chief Scientist; Magician and part time Jester; Howard's Multiverse associate.
- **Otto the Magnificent – aka Hairy Otter** – An absolutely terrible illusionist magician, Otto the Magnificent escaped the claws of super villain Imperius Drake but not before he developed some amazing powers courtesy of Imperius' genetic alterations.
- **L.Condor** – Andean Condor; cybernet genius with a twelve-foot wingspan and artificial voice. Chief Technical Officer (CTO) of the Advanced Super Computing Center-Deep Data Hexagon

- **Chita** – Cheetah – Beautiful, fascinating, clever, sexy, immoral and highly independent feline – among other things, publisher and editor-in-chief of *PURR* and *SOW* magazines and Director of UUI Media.
- **Benedict and Galatea Tigris**, the Flying Tigers, twin sibling white Bengals – Pilots of the Octavian Air Force.
- **Merow** – Emperor of Orient on Exoplanet Orb.
- **Empress Catrin** – Wife of Merow.
- **Apricot** – Their Daughter.
- **Dowager Empress** – Merow's Mother.
- **Leonidas** – High Priest on Exoplanet Orb.
- **Magister Purre** – Minister to the Emperor on Exoplanet Orb.
- **Gaston** – Great Pyrenees Sheep Dog – New Orleans Drug Lord.
- **Luciano** – Neapolitan Mastiff – Undercover agent for the FBI.
- **Special Agent Honey Badger** – FBI.
- **Lord Portnoy Porcupine** – Chief Executive Rhea Governing Council.
- **Priscilla Porcupine** – Director Rhea Science Center.
- **General Bill Bison** – Rhea Defense Councilor.
- **Roger Raccoon** – Rhea Hotelier.
- **Grigor Gregory** – Grizzly Bear – Director of the Gaean Telcom Center.
- **Jill Gazelle** – Grigor's Personal Assistant.
- **Harvey Wise** – Homo Sapiens – Satellite Launch Director.
- **Marie Leonore** – Lioness – Vice President of Gaea.
- **Jim Wiley** – H.Sap – Gaean Legislator.
- **Laura Fisher** – H.Sap – Gaean Legislator.
- **Edward Equid** – Horse – Gaean Defense Secretary.
- **Dougal** – Shetland Sheep Dog – Estate Manager of Polar Paradise.
- **Lord David** – Dalmatian Dog – Former Chamberlain to the Exiled King.
- **Dancing Dan** – Boxer – Lord David's Bodyguard and Personal Trainer.
- **Flame** – An Extraordinary Fire Engine.
- **Jaguar Jack the Lad** – Longtime Compadre of Octavius Bear.
- **Ms. Fairbearn** – Canadian Polar – Chief Housekeeper of Bearmoral Castle / Polar Paradise.
- **Bearmoral Shetland Sheep: Dolly, Holly, Molly and Polly** – Housemaids, Lounge Waitresses and probable Clones.
- **Mrs. McRadish** – Sheep – Chief Cook at Polar Paradise.
- **Fiona** – Dandie Dinmont Terrier – Lounge Manager at Polar Paradise.
- **Lion and Unicorn** – Owners of the Baltasound pub of the same name.
- **Harold** – Sea Otter – manages the castle's beaches, pools and watercraft.

- **Chief Inspector Bruce Wallaroo** – Irrepressible but brilliant marsupial; an international law and order genius from Down Under; currently assigned to Interpol; assists Octavius and Maury.
- **Tilda Roo** – associate of Bruce Wallaroo. Former Melbourne detective.
- **Byzz – Byzantia Bonobo** – Chief Ursula Developer.
- **Ursula 13 and 14** – Universal Ursine Intellect Systems.
- **Huntley** – Siberian Husky – Bear's Lair Butler.

<u>Locations</u>

Cincinnati, Ohio; UUI, Kentucky; New Orleans; Polar Paradise, the Shetlands; The Multiverse – Orb; Rhea; Gaea

Octavius

Prologue

Do Bears give you a scare? Well, me too!
So, I'll pass on this tactic to you.
You just fix that old Bear
With a cold, piercing stare.
But make sure that he's Winnie-the-Pooh.

Hello again or first-time greetings to new readers of the Casebooks of Octavius Bear. I am Mauritius (Maury) Meerkat, sidekick to Octavius Bear and your genial host and narrator of this series. Delighted to welcome you to Volume Seventeen -*The Octavian Cases.*

Before we launch off into our next adventure, a few introductions are in order. Octavius and I; our two magnificent Wolf associates, Frau Ilse Schuylkill and Colonel Wyatt Where; our resident all-round talent, Otto the Magnificent and Huntley Husky, our Butler are all present and accounted for at the Bear's Lair, his opulent estate on the Ohio River near Cincinnati.

Readers of Books 14, 15 and 16 are aware that Senhor L. Condor (Condo) is now our Chief Technical Officer (CTO) – Advanced Super Computing Center-UUI. He's in Kentucky at the huge Deep Data Hexagon complex advancing the fortunes of the Center. Byzantia Bonobo is managing the Ursula program and hard at work developing Ursula 14.

Our scientific geniuses, Howard Watt and Marlin the Dolphin, are at the Bear's Lair running our Multiverse Project.

We're awaiting the arrival of Bearoness Belinda Béarnaise Bruin Bear *(nee Black)*, Octavius' wife and the Twins mother. Upon her return from Australia, *(Book 16)* she headed off with their super-precocious Twins, Arabella and McTavish. to the Shetlands for a brief stay at her castle/resort, Polar Paradise. The Twins are now officially Juveniles. They returned from Down Under full of ideas, requests, stories and energy. *(See Volume 16-The Cases Down Under.)* Also on board the Aquabear SST is Mlle Woof, a unique and highly capable Bichon Frisé. You'll meet her again.

Bearoness Belinda
Béarnaise Bruin
(nee Black)

Belinda, in order to retain her Bearonial status, must occupy her castle in Scotland at least six months of the year. She and Octavius do high speed commutes between their spectacular homes in Cincinnati and the Shetlands. Today she's flying back via the Aquabear, the last SST Concorde aloft. On this run, the plane is piloted by Benedict and Galatea Tigris, the Flying Tigers, twin sibling white Bengals. She is accompanied by the Juveniles, Mlle Giselle Woof and Chita, whom they picked up in London.

Maury Meerkat

As I said, my name is Maury Meerkat – also known as Offscreen Narrator. When I am part of the action, I am Octavius' trusted associate and field captain. I am two feet tall plus tail and I weigh in at twenty-four pounds. He, on the other hand, is a huge Alaskan Kodiak – over nine feet tall, weighing 1400 pounds – and like many of his species, given to emotional outbursts.

As you may already know, Octavius prides himself on his many skills in the fields of biology, physics, ursinology, voodoo, teleology, chemistry, apiculture, and oenology. He is a self-made gazillionaire and, in spite of the late Caleb Cassowary's abortive attempt in Book 14 to unseat him, still sole owner of UUI *(Universal Ursine Industries.)* He is also a first rate electrical, electronic, structural, marine, computer, communications, aeronautical, civil, mechanical, aerospace and chemical engineer. He has a few other interesting characteristics such as falling into brief, deep narcoleptic comas – side effects of his successful genetic experiments to eliminate the need for him to hibernate.

However, the talent and occupation that should interest you most is his avocation for criminology. The Bear often works in close concert with Inspector Bruce Wallaroo from Australia and Interpol, and with his own Cincinnati and Shetlands based team – The Octavians.

When we are not out scouring the world for evildoers, in cooperation with local, national and international constabularies, we are primarily headquartered in the Bear's Lair, a rambling old mansion near Cincinnati which encompasses not only the Great Bear's opulent digs, but his massive laboratories and shops; his missile silo disguised as an Asian pagoda; *(Don't ask!)* and a giant Roman temple that serves as a hangar for his four airplanes: a Twin Otter; a F15E Strike Eagle; a V-22 Osprey; a C5A-The Ursa Major; plus an AgustaWestland AW101 VVIP luxury helicopter -The Ursa Minor. Why so many? Ask him!

Across the Ohio River in Northern Kentucky, sit the headquarters, labs and some production facilities of Universal Ursine Industries (UUI). Further west is the fantastic Deep Data Hexagon, home of the UUI Advanced Super Computing Center under the direction of Senhor L. Condor (Condo.) Our story will take us there periodically.

Now let me take a moment and further introduce a highly essential and near-miraculous member of the Octavians – Ursula – Universal Ursine Intellect Model 13 – Artificial General Intelligence System. I'll let her explain herself.

"Thank you, Maury. Hello everyone!! My official nomenclature is Universal Ursine Intellect Model 13–Artificial General Intelligence System (AGI). Ursula 13 for short. My predecessor systems and I were developed by the Advanced Super Computing Center of UUI. I am the result of the Computing Center team using those earlier versions to create a further enhanced entity – me, the Model 13, which, we hope will help produce even more sophisticated, independent and powerful AGI systems in the near future. Each advanced unit contains the capabilities, memories and power of its progenitors so in a sense, we are not replacing but rather expanding the Ursula family. During the Caleb Cassowary era, Model 13 was temporarily shelved. He's gone and I am now in full operation and Ursula 14 is under development."

"While I am physically supported by a highly secure and hyper-powered server farm at the Kentucky Hexagon, I also exist independently in clouds and network-based nodes and can be simultaneously incorporated into a wide variety of separate devices like this laptop unit. I combine quantum computing elements with extremely high speed conventional circuits. I have practically limitless data capacity and 5G+ transmission speed. My super high-velocity multi-tasking abilities and algorithms allow me to continuously serve an exceptionally large number of entities while simultaneously and autonomously enhancing my own capabilities. Ursula 14 will be equipped with Virtual and Augmented Reality capabilities."

"Depending on the physical unit in which I'm housed, I can see, hear, feel and smell. I speak and understand an almost infinite number of languages and dialects. I can change my appearance and my vocal output to suit most moods and situations. I can interact with other devices, vehicles and structures and of course, all varieties of sentient animals in this world."

"I am also an important component of the Multiverse Project and I adapt my capabilities to deal with alternate universes as they are discovered.

I have restraining functions which prevent me from doing deliberate harm even in self-defense, unless I am released by a recognized authority using very carefully protected clandestine codes. Finally, I have been told that although the Ursulas are shy on emotions, I have developed a finely-honed sense of humor. LOL!"

Ursula has other highly important capabilities that we don't talk about publicly such as creating and breaking all known encryption codes and piercing deep personal identification techniques.

Our team no longer believes she is magical or supernatural. I'm not sure what she is. Her personality gets more independent and socially adept every day and she has taken to anticipating our interactions with ease and accuracy. Needless to say, for security purposes, we conceal her existence to all but a very few individuals with a need to know. She is also highly skilled in self-protection.

As we move along in our literary safari, you'll have ample opportunity to meet the other Bear's Lair stars of our previous outings - Frau Schuylkill and her mate, Colonel Wyatt Where (Ret.); Chita aka Madame Catt; Otto the Magnificent (Hairy Otter); Senhor L. Condor (Condo); Howard Watt and Marlin; Chief Inspector Bruce Wallaroo and let's not forget Mlle Woof and Huntley Husky.

You'll also encounter the Shetlands crew housed at Polar Paradise and Baltasound.

*****

At the close of Volume Fifteen - *A Case for the Birds*, Octavius and his lovely wife Belinda made a major decision.

She proposed, "I think it's time we both retired. When you had your last business review with Griselda, *(UUI President and COO)* the other officers, directors and managers, it occurred to me that they had everything in Universal Ursine Industries pretty much under control. Business was growing. With the exception of the Caleb induced lawsuits, there are very few downsides. What a perfect opportunity to step aside, relax, travel with Arabella and McTavish and just enjoy life."

"No more criminals, cranks or despots. You can become a 'Consulting Detective Emeritus'. We can spend more time at Polar Paradise but of course, we won't give up the Bear's Lair and we can go to fun places. There's a lot of world out there I want to see, to say nothing of other worlds. I've never quantum jumped and I'd like to."

Octavius sat with his mouth open. "Wow!"

"Tavi, is that all you have to say. Wow?"

"Frankly, my dear, I've never considered retiring."

"I know. You believe you're indispensable. The Ursine in Universal Ursine. The Octavius at the head of the Octavians. But Maury, Howard, Marlin, Otto, the Wolves and Condo all are super capable. The Ursulas are wonders and getting more so every day. Chita, Mlle Woof, the Colonel and Bruce are fabulous. Huntley and Ilse have the Lair running like a well-oiled machine. Dougal and his staff along with Lord David and Dancing Dan manage Polar Paradise to perfection. Tavi, we're not getting any younger. I'm tired of being a sidekick Bearoness and frankly, I'm bored stiff with the Aquabears. Let's do something different."

"What about the Cubs, excuse me, the Juveniles?"

"They can turn their Internet games over to the Hexagon team and come along with us as we roam. They'll love it. We'll take complete charge of them. Poor Mlle Woof can stay here and relax. Well, what do you say?"

"The idea has its appeal, I'm bored, too. This last round with Home World, Caleb and General Turmoil really flattened my fur. Tell you what, Bel. Let's sneak up on it. We'll take a one year sabbatical and see what we think at the end. An experiment. No bridges burned. The bad guys will still have the Octavian team to contend with. No permanent farewells. No cold turkey, whatever that means. Things won't be exactly the same when we come back but we could resume, if we want to. We'd still own all the assets and titles. How about that for a start?"

"OK! It's my idea but I must admit to having a few trepidations, too. Slow and easy! We can keep our home bases here and in the Shetlands. We'll use the Concorde SST. Let's see if the Flying Tigers are up to being global wanderers."

The shockwave among the Octavians wasn't as intense as they thought it would be. In fact, Chita's reaction was "What took you so long?"

I was invited to come along on their odyssey but I declined, saying I might join them from time to time. Howard said he stood ready to arrange Multiverse trips when they wanted them. Belinda agreed eagerly but thought an Earth bound trip should be number one. First stop-Australia. *(See Book 16 - The Cases Down Under)*

Frau Schuylkill, the ever astute she-wolf, summed it up. "Go, have an adventure for yourselves. We'll keep things rolling along and we'll know how to reach you if we have to. It's not as if you don't have a highly competent staff, associates and infrastructure. You built it, now enjoy the fruits."

The Twins *(juveniles)* were delighted. They'd be World *(Universe)* travelers! Yes!! They turned their Internet game-The Bold Brave Brilliant Bumptious Bears over to a group of gamester geeks at the Deep Data Hexagon, secure in the knowledge that its features and popularity would continue to grow in their year long absence.

Mlle. Woof was of two minds. She would miss the youngsters but she could use some rest. For the time being. she was going to stay at Polar Paradise in the Shetlands along with the resort staff. *(She wouldn't relax for very long.)*

In Scotland, Belinda's hotel and castle was running at almost full capacity under the watchful eyes of Dougal – Shetland Sheep Dog Estate Manager; Ms. Fairbearn – Chief Housekeeper; Mrs. McRadish – Chief Cook; The Security team of Lord David, Dancing Dan and Flame, their Fire Engine; Dolly, Holly, Molly and Polly – Sheep Housemaids, Lounge Waitresses and probable Clones; Harold – Sea Otter in charge of the castle's beaches, pools and watercraft. Harold had just become the overseer of two jetskis and kayaks, courtesy of the Twins' love affair with them on the Great Barrier Reef in Australia.

Let's not forget Lion and Unicorn – Proprietors of the Baltasound pub of the same name and Fiona – Dandie Dinmont Terrier – their Lounge Manager at Polar Paradise. Keeping the alcoholic ambrosia flowing.

It went without saying that along with her other assignments, an Ursula would go with Octavius and Belinda wherever they went. They'd grown to rely on those electronic wonders. She'll also be recording and relaying their adventures so I can pass them on to you.

Now, Belinda and the Twins were back at the Bear's Lair and ready for a Multiverse jaunt. Truth be told, so was Octavius. Chita wasn't interested. "I'm an earth-bound critter."

Howard had been observing all this. The porcupine grinned. "Are you four up for another adventure? Have you decompressed from your trip Down Under? Marlin and I have found a new exoplanet that we think is worth a trip. Otto has given it a preliminary look-see. Sentient civilized animals, breathable air, reasonable climate, no homo sapiens, reptiles or paranoid birds. Thought you and the Twins might be interested."

"I thought we'd start you off with a pretty benign environment. Our prior intergalactic sojourns have been stimulating *(for which read 'dangerous')* to say the least. Although your recent earthly adventures haven't been cakewalks, either."

Since Octavius got involved in two murders, bid rigging, extortion, money laundering, an attempted mugging, a traffic accident and fierce monsoon storms in Australia, his 'retirement' so far was hardly tranquil. Maybe a trip off-world would be different. He hoped so.

"What do you think, Bel?"

"Sounds good to me. I think the kids will love it although they're a bit jaded from their trip down under."

"They've still got a healthy supply of enthusiasm. OK, Howard. Let's do it."

(Sorry, it took so long to get started with the action but I wanted to give you the lay of the land. So, let's end this Prologue and get on with ...)

Chapter One

The Octavians head out to space.
Planet Orb is their first stopping place.
Both the Twins are psyched-out
But Belinda's in doubt.
Could this lead to another weird case?

First thing on the agenda. Determine whether or not the travelers are "adepts" – that is, can they engage in Multiverse travel directly without benefit of a portable transit device? It is a genetic quirk. Some animals could and some couldn't. Octavius could and did. Howard and Otto could. I couldn't. What about the Twins and Belinda?

Marlin had developed a test procedure for establishing their abilities. A quantum motion trip simulator. Candidates were attached to an array of sensors that could detect whether they were capable of direct Multiverse transit. The Twins went first. Arabella – green lights across the panel. McTavish, the same. High fives from the Furball Adepts.

Next up – Belinda. She got strapped in. Howard threw the switch. No response. The Twins winced. "What's wrong, Howard? Shouldn't the panel light up?" Marlin looked out through his glass container and laughed. The Bearoness' ornaments were interfering with the signal. "Milady, I'm afraid you're going to have to take off your gold and jewelry items. The simulator doesn't like them."

Rings, earrings, bracelets, a necklace and a coronet all came tumbling on the table. "Okay, guys, let's try again."

Still nothing. Head scratching, embarrassed looks. Then McTavish came out with an emphatic "Yess!! Mom, you forgot the ankle bracelet."

"Oh dear, so I did. Alright. One more time!"

Bingo, Green lights all the way.

"Does that mean I can't wear my jewelry when we transport?"

"No, just when you're simulating. It's a glitch in our system."

Octavius snorted, "Fine. That means we can all travel unimpeded without a transit device. Tell us about this place, Howard."

Otto had been standing by watching the tests. "I've been there, chief. Albeit very briefly. It's pretty benevolent. Orbits a solar-type star along with two other uninhabited planets. Rather small but definitely livable. Breathable air, a flourishing agriculture and water. Rivers, lakes and one ocean."

Howard picked up. "A modest population of sentient mammals. They seem quite intelligent, however. They speak a semi-recognizable language but I sometimes had to use Ursula to make myself understood. You'll be pleased to know there are fish but no reptiles and definitely no birds."

"That's a relief. Does this planet have a name?"

"They call it Orb."

"They may be intelligent but they're not very original. What kind of mammals, Otto?"

"As far as I know, there are no homo sapiens but I can't be definite about that. I didn't see any."

"Would you know one if you met one?"

"Oh, you bet. I did spot some bovines, felines, canines, mustelae, deer, a few other ruminants and are you ready for this, ursines."

Arabella chortled. "Oh goody! We won't be the only bears."

"Hmm! Who's in charge. What kind of government do they have?"

Ursula picked up on that. "There are actually two major regions. East Orb and West. They are separated by the Great Ocean. Each area has very little to do with each other. Communication on the planet is rather primitive, transportation is basic and very little commerce or interaction takes place between the two regions. The country names translate into Orient and Occident. Interesting! It's as if they were actually on two different planets."

"The Orient where I landed has a semi-religious system of government, not unlike ancient Egypt, the Incas or some mid-eastern countries today. An emperor who is treated as a demi-god. In this case, a cat-like animal called a Merow. Based on my short exposure, he does not seem

24

to be a tyrant. In fact, his rule seems to be quite altruistic. As you might expect under such a system he is surrounded by courtiers and priests. Probably the usual palace intrigues, chicanery, pushing and shoving for position and influence going on in the background. We've seen that before."

"The Occident, on the other side of the Great Ocean, is small, tribal and nomadic led by independent chieftains. Very religious but worshipping different gods. I don't know much more about them than that. Like some countries in Earth's Middle East. They have little to do with the Orient."

Howard intervened. "We plan to land in the Orient. Otto made contact with several royal councilors and convinced them that he was from a distant planet circling a star similar to their own. He called it Mediana. He told them he was an advance animal for a small aristocratic delegation arriving shortly on a cosmic Grand Tour. He was their staff magician."

Otto picked it back up. "The councilors were dubious but the Merow bought Otto's story after he 'zapped' and reappeared several times and moved a few items telekinetically. He's eager to meet with you all."

"The citizens of Orb have no concept of galactic quantum travel. We must be vague about our origins and nature. By general agreement here in the Multiverse community, we can't tamper with the development of other planets and civilizations. If they make discoveries themselves, that's OK."

Belinda sniffed, "This is beginning to sound complicated and even dangerous. Tavi, what do you think?"

Octavius pawsed for a moment. "Just remember, Bel, if it gets nasty in any way we can jump back to Earth in a flash. Marlin and Ursula will be tracking us 24/7. We signal and we vamoose. It should be interesting and very educational for the Twins. Do you two agree?"

McTavish laughed, "Mom, Australia got complicated and dangerous. I want to see this place. How about you, Bella?"

"I'm excited. I never thought I would ever travel to another planet. This one sounds fascinating with all the differences. We could build another game around it when we return. Bears in Space. With Maury, Marlin, Ursula, Howard and Otto all watching our backs, we should be fine."

McTavish laughed, "Maybe we should have an escape drill like they do on ships. Running back to Earth after we arrive. Remember what we did on the superyacht in Australia. Maybe I could learn to 'zap' like Otto."

The Otter laughed. "First you'd have to meet up with a deranged Duck like I did. Imperius Drake and his handy hypodermics."

"No thanks. I'll pass on that experience. So, what do you think, Mom?"

Belinda smiled. "Well I was the one who wanted the quantum travel experience so I can hardly back down and none of the other exoplanets the team has already explored sound all that attractive. OK Howard, let's do it."

"Fine. Pack light. We can always send for stuff if we need it. We'll leave tomorrow morning."

Otto said, "You'll need your jewelry, Bearoness. You'll be meeting up with royalty. The Merow has a wife, Empress Catrin and a daughter. I think she's called Apricot. But she's away at school. Sorry, kids! His mother, The Dowager Empress lives at the palace. Interesting lady!"

"Well, I've rubbed shoulders with monarchs and royalty before. Being a Bearoness has its plusses. So has Octavius for that matter. Haven't you, Tavi?"

Before he could answer, McTavish blurted, "Tell her about the Prince of Whales, Dad."

"Your mother knows all about the Prince. Remember, that's how we got Marlin. He's on a hopefully permanent loan to us from the Prince or until he wants to go back. "

"Ooh right! Sorry, Marlin! I forgot. Are you going to leave?"

"Think nothing of it, young bear. No, I'm not leaving. I may want to travel a bit, though. This tank can get boring. Howard and I have discussed it. We'll see. Enjoy your voyage."

"We will! We will!"

Chapter Two

Off they go on their first Quantum hop.
Both the Twins and their Kodiak Pop.
Bel and Otto add two.
Howard rounds out the crew.
And there's Ursula in her laptop.

Maury here. Next morning, The Octavians crowded into the Multiverse Lab to see the cosmic travelers off on their journey to Orb and the country of Orient. The tourists agreed their stories would stick pretty closely to their actual situation. Earth would be known as Mediana. The Bearoness was a member of Mediana nobility *(which she is)*. Octavius was her formidable consort. The Twins were the reason for the tour. Part of their education. Howard was the group's organizer and facilitator. Otto was her staff magician. Ursula was Otto's familiar spirit. She took on the visage of a black cat for the duration. She would seldom appear, if at all.

They would tell the Orienters *(not Orientals)* that they were capable of inter-stellar travel but were forbidden by their gods from revealing how they carried it off. No space ship, angels, fiery chariot or flying machine. Otto could 'zap' them all elsewhere at a moment's notice and Marlin could bring them back to Earth *(Mediana)* in a flash. They were eager to meet the Emperor Merow *(which they were.)*

Hugs and good wishes all around. Last minute instructions from the Bearoness. Promises by the Twins to bring back souvenirs. Emotional embraces by Mlle Woof. They'd be back in a few weeks.

Howard got them positioned on the take-off mat and Marlin turned on the transmitter/tracker. A hum, a whoosh and they disappeared. Marlin watched the digital display as it followed their almost instant progress. A chime sounded and the screen indicated they had arrived safely. We applauded. Frau Schuylkill looked around. "Any one for breakfast?" Chita looked up over her bowl of coffee. "Well, Maury. We got them launched on another trip. I hope it's calmer than their Aussie run. Meanwhile, what do we do for an encore?"

The Development of Civilization Volume 17
Part 2
Special Agents and Detectives
From "An Introduction to Faunapology"

by Octavius Bear Ph.D.

A _Special Agent_ is an investigator or detective for a governmental or independent agency, who primarily serves in criminal investigatory positions. Additionally, many federal and state "Special Agents" operate in "criminal intelligence" based roles as well.

Most people holding the title of "Special Agent" are law enforcement officers under state or federal law (with some also being dual intelligence operatives such as with the FBI). These law enforcement officers are distinctly empowered to conduct both major and minor criminal investigations and hold arrest authority.

Additionally, most Special Agents are authorized to carry firearms both on and off duty due to their status as law enforcement officers. In US federal law enforcement, the title of "Special Agent" is used almost exclusively for federal and military criminal investigators.

A _Detective_ is an investigator, usually a member of a law enforcement agency. They often collect information to solve crimes by talking to witnesses and informants, collecting physical evidence, or searching records in databases. This leads them to arrest criminals and enable them to be convicted in court. A detective may work for the police or privately as I do. Octavius Bear – Consulting Detective.

Informally, a detective is a licensed or unlicensed person who solves offenses, including historical crimes, by examining and evaluating clues and personal records in order to uncover the identity and/or whereabouts of criminals. Some, like me, are private persons, and may be known as private investigators, or shortened to simply "private eyes".

That defines the Octavians. We are usually known to work in close coordination with members of law enforcement, worldwide. Two of our major contacts are Chief Inspector Bruce Wallaroo of Interpol and the Australian Federal Police and Special Agent Honey Badger of the FBI.

*****

"Don't worry, Chita. Something will happen shortly. It always does."

Out of the mouths of meerkats! After checking in with Marlin and Ursula several times to see how the Grand Tourists were doing, I settled down in the lounge to catch up on my theatrical agent's workload. Residuals to administer; income for the Twins' games; roles for Bearyl and Bearnice Blanc, actress and singer, respectively – Belinda's former twin polar sidekicks; offers of gigs for Chita, Belinda, the Twins, Lord David and Flame and an inquiry about using Polar Paradise for a series. There was also a request for Lion and Unicorn. My client list had grown substantially.

My cell phone rang and a Zoom connection came on. Special Agent Honey Badger – FBI. Hadn't spoken to her in a while. "Hello, Meerkat! How are all the Octavians? I heard from Bruce Wallaroo that your Boss had an interesting set of sessions in Australia recently. Is he up to doing a little work for the FBI? I tried to reach him but he's incommunicado."

"Hi, Special Agent Badger. He and his family are off world for the next few weeks. *(She was Multiverse savvy, especially after the Caleb Cassowary fiasco.)* Most of the Octavians are here. Is there any way we can help? I've been left in charge."

She pawsed for a moment and then said, "Yeah, why not. You guys do most of Octavius' heavy lifting after all. *(a snicker)* We have a rather unusual problem that's as much in your line as ours. Calls for a bit of undercover work by animals unknown to the underworld. Preferably female."

"Okay, let me round up Chita and Frau Schuylkill and we'll call you back. Belinda's off on the galactic tour with Octavius. Galatea Tigris, one of our pilots is also here."

"Fine! I'll wait to hear from you."

I hung up and set about contacting the ladies. This sounded like it could be interesting. The Octavians ride again – at least the Femme Private Eyes.

I was greeted with a bark from the other side of the room. Mlle Woof."

"Maury, I couldn't help overhearing your conversation with the FBI Agent. I'm a female, unknown and currently underemployed. The Twins are off on another jaunt and really, they don't need a governess any more. I want to earn my keep. I need something to do."

"Gosh, Mlle Woof. It didn't occur to me. I've always associated you with the Twins full time. I guess you're right. We certainly want you to stay."

"Merci! Please call me Giselle. I don't suppose you are aware that some of the most skilled detective animals came from France. Jules Maigret, Arsène Lupin, Vidocq, C. August Dupin. There are females too. Aimee Leduc, Candace Renoir, Catherine LeVendeur."

"Oh sure! Hercule Poirot, Clouseau!"

"Non, non. Poirot is a Belgian ferret and Clouseau is a canine fool."

"Oh, Sorry! Okay Mlle er, Giselle. Let me call in Chita and Ilse and we'll get a hold of Galatea, too."

A few fast cell calls and the Octavian Femme Private Eyes were sitting with me in a conference room in front of a webcam equipped desk top.

"Ladies. How many of you are interested in doing a little detective work for the FBI. I don't know what it is yet but I understand from Special Agent Honey Badger that it involves undercover work, preferably by a female. They all raised their paws but Chita seemed to hesitate. "Maury, you know about my history with Imperius Drake. And remember, I actually killed him. The less I usually have to do with law enforcement, the better."

I pondered, "In this case, that history might be an advantage. We'll see. I'm sure Agent Badger knows about your days with the despicable Duck."

Chita, Ilse and Galatea looked a bit surprised to see Mlle Woof in the group without the Twins in tow. She smiled and said, "With no Twins to chase, I'm looking for someone else to go after."

They laughed. "Good for you, Mamselle!"

"Please call me Giselle. Mlle Woof is only for the Twins."

"Okay," I said, "I'm going to call Agent Badger."

The Zoom call went through and The Badger appeared. The white stripe down the center of her grey head led past two piercing eyes to a twitching snout. A threatening stare, no doubt practiced in front of a mirror to cause no end of discomfort to her victims. She announced herself. "Special Agent Badger. Oh Hi, Maury!" The frown disappeared and she actually smiled. "Thanks for getting back so quickly. Are these our candidates? Hello Ladies. I know two of you. Chita and Frau Schuylkill."

"Let me introduce you to the other two. Galatea Tigris, Gal to her friends, is one of Bearoness Belinda's pilots. The Bearoness is off world at the moment so her flight crew is at leisure. You know Frau Schuylkill is also a pilot and ex-military. This other lady, Mlle Giselle Woof, a Bichon Frisé, is probably unknown to you. She has been the governess of the Twins pretty much since their birth but she is looking to call up her other skills."

"What skills are those, Giselle?"

"Monsieur Maury does not know this but I had a short career as a stage actress in France before going to work for the Bearoness and Doctor Bear. I'm an acrobat and I know judo. Nobody ever suspects a small, cute, curly haired dog of being able to defend herself. This puppy cut makes me look younger than I am. And, of course, I speak French."

"Did you ever act here in the States?"

"Non!"

I intervened, "I'm a part time theatrical agent and I didn't know she was a thespian."

"Good. So you're not likely to be known among the group we're going after. Chita, you're famous and infamous. You might be at risk. Gal, you're intimidating. I think you'd scare these guys but Giselle, you can play the innocent, little white Gallic dog routine and Frau Schuylkill, you speak French and German. If you can shed your military appearance and look exotic, I think you two would make the team we want."

I asked, "How about telling us what it is you have in mind. I don't want these ladies getting hurt or worse yet, getting killed"

31

Mlle Giselle Woof   Galatea Tigris

Frau Schuylkill   Chita

The Octavian "Femme Private Eyes"

(There was actually another female or cyber female in the room. Another manifestation of Ursula. The multi-tasking AGI was in passive mode picking up the conversation and recording it for future playback and review. The Ursulas were getting their exercise while the Bears were away.)

The Special Agent went on. "Okay, here's the situation. Down in New Orleans, a major drug running business is in full swing managed by a group of European illegals. We call it The French Connection II. A Great Pyrenees dog named Gaston Le Chien is in charge. We want him captured, jailed or deported and his operation shut down. The Coast Guard, ICE, Homeland Security, DEA, the FBI and local police all have made dents in his activities. We've intercepted large shipments of pills and arrested a number of his workers, including mules but he keeps eluding us. He knows all our operatives and is on extreme guard against us." The Frau shook her head. "What do you expect two female canines to do that you haven't already attempted?"

"Gaston has a vulnerability. He is extremely superstitious. He believes in voodoo, phantoms, ghosts, spirits and apparitions. He attends seances and seeks out fortune tellers and seers. We want you to come on the scene and play oracles. Because of your abilities with foreign languages and your Continental backgrounds, my management thinks we can lead him into a trap. You're also both quite attractive and you, Giselle, are a former actress. Frau Ilse, your military background and sharpshooting is a major plus,."

"We want you to work independently, even competitively. It will give you both more credibility when you tell him the same things and lead him into our trap. Are you willing?"

I squeaked, "Wait a second. These guys are dangerous. What are you going to do to protect these two so-called oracles?"

"We're importing agents from other cities to act as clandestine bodyguards. The ladies will be under constant surveillance and protection."

Frau Ilse said, "We need to have our own protection, too. Not that I don't trust the FBI but the Octavians are used to providing their own security."

Chapter Three

The Octavian Femme Private eyes
Will play soothsayers in a disguise.
They will practice their guile
On a mad Francophile
While the tourists on Orb socialize.

Ilse laughed. "Okay, I'll do it but I want my mate, Colonel Wyatt Where. By the way, my hyperspeed abilities may come in handy. Maury, when is Otto returning? Can we get him to join the party and look after Giselle?"

The Bichon frowned, "I'm not sure I need looking after. Especially by Otto."

I replied, "Otto is not the goof he makes himself out to be. He's a formidable animal with those special telekinetic skills you're aware of. He can also 'zap' you out of danger in a microsecond. He was supposed to come back once they got the Bears established on the planet Orb. Howard was going to remain and manage the program."

Mlle Woof giggled, "Well, I wanted something different to do rather than baby-sit the grown up Twins. This is certainly different. Frau Ilse and Madame Giselle. Mystics! Besides, I'll have Galatea with me, won't I."

The white tiger who had been listening to all this nodded her massive head.

The Bichon barked, "D'accord! Let's go."

"I'll check on Otto's status. By the way, Agent Badger, each one of our soothsayers will have an Ursula with them at all times."

"Great. I have some arrangements to make. Be back soon."

*****

Meanwhile on the exoplanet Orb, the Space Tourists had landed at an agreed upon site preselected by Otto and planetary authorities. They were checking each other out. A small contingent of imperial feline retainers approached the group, recognized the Otter and extended salutations.

(Henceforth, Ursula will simultaneously translate all conversations on Orb and will pass them on to you directly, Dear Reader. Much simpler than struggling with language interpretation issues.)

Their leader bowed and said, "Good day, Master Magician Otto. We have been watching the agreed upon landing site for you and your entourage. Welcome all to Orb and Orient. The Merow sends his greetings and asks that you accompany us to the Imperial Palace. We hope your journey was serene, swift and fruitful. It is beyond our understanding how you travel among the stars and planets but we understand that you have been forbidden by your gods to share that information. We see no vehicle and so we conclude you travel by personal magic."

Otto replied, "Thank you, Magister Purre, it is good to see you again. Please accept our gratitude for your gracious assistance and the Emperor's permission to visit your planet and country. Thank you also for accepting the restrictions we have laid upon us by our gods. When we reach the Merow, I shall introduce the members of our party."

A short walk to a magnificent structure set in the middle of a tree-laden grove. The Imperial Palace! Groups of richly clad animals, not dissimilar in appearance to the denizens of Earth, stared at the six travelers along the route. Octavius switched from walking on all fours to moving erect, demonstrating his nine foot height and substantial girth. Pure white Belinda, as usual, attracted much attention. She was adorned with her bearonial jewelry. The Twins who were also unusual, got their share of scrutiny. Otto had redonned his red wizard's costume and Howard remained in the background.

Belinda asked, "How does one address his Imperial Majesty?"

The magister replied, " 'Your Majesty' is correct and quite sufficient. He is not given to extravagant titles or royal flourishes."

She replied, "An attitude to which I heartily subscribe."

At the opulent entrance to the Palace, several guards, richly uniformed in blue and gold, bowed, opened the portals and stood aside. The Magister and his associates led the way inside through a series of high ceilinged anterooms decorated with classical paintings and statuary to a pair of tall, golden doors embellished with feline images. Another pair of soldiers stood guard. One opened the portal, stepped inside, bowed respectfully in the direction of a throne a significant distance away and intoned loudly, "Your Majesty, Magister Purre, members of the court and your visitors requesting an audience."

A powerful feline voice responded, "Splendid, Show them in."

The Merow was seated on a gold emblazoned throne, wearing a crown and richly embroidered robes. A jewel encrusted staff leaned against the seat. He held a booklet in his lap taken from a small stack lying on a table covered with a velvet cloth. A pad and pen rested nearby.

He was impressive, indeed. The thought flashed though Belinda's mind. If her movie producer friend, Preston Pavel Polar was looking for a royal figure right out of Central Casting for one of his films, this guy was it. Tall, with face and paws covered in blue-grey fur, his large feline eyes swept the group as they entered. His whiskers quivered as his mouth broke into a smile.

He spoke with an uncharacteristic rumble. "Pardon me for a moment while I dispose of these decrees in need of my signature and paw print.'

He placed his left paw on the pad and then the page of the open booklet. He then took up the pen and in rapid strokes, signed his name. He repeated this process several times until the stack had been exhausted.

He gestured for Magister Purre to take up the documents and get them prepared for reproduction and distribution. The courtier left the room loaded down with parchment.

The Merow nodded. "He'll be back shortly. Good, that's over. I hate paperwork. Now we can socialize. Welcome earthlings!"

OTTO THE MAGNIFICENT

Chapter Four

The two psychics are learning their parts
In performing the card reading arts.
Many light years away,
The High Priest has his say
And a nasty encounter soon starts.

Maury here. Back on Earth at the Bear's Lair. Preparing for Mlle Giselle Woof and Frau Schuylkill to take up temporary residence in New Orleans as practitioners of the occult arts. The Bichon will occupy a small pied-à-terre in the artsy Warehouse District while Frau Ilse establishes herself in a hotel in the French Quarter. The FBI has acquired these two locations through a local agent unknown *(we hope)* to Gaston Le Chien.

Scenario: The two psychics are aware of each other and are avowed competitors. Madame Giselle is a long-standing Louisiana resident who just changed her domicile to New Orleans from Baton Rouge while the Frau is on a national tour. Hopefully, that will explain their recent arrivals on the Big Easy scene. Gaston keeps himself updated on all things occult and will be informed of the two mediums' arrival in town. During a series of readings both of them will allude to the arrival of a potential Mexican challenger *(an actor)* intent on taking over Gaston's business. With luck, Gaston, with his hair trigger temper *(no pun)* will himself seek out this rival and attempt to do him in. He'll be arrested on an attempted murder charge. The clairvoyants will quietly leave the scene and return to Cincinnati.

Yes, law enforcement knows this caper could be interpreted as entrapment but Gaston is no innocent. They hope it will set off destructive clashes within his mob as they fight to replace the boss. Nothing like a good old fashioned gang war. Well that's the plan. Let's see how it pans out.

Ilse and the Colonel would be together. He was acting as her assistant and bodyguard although the ex-military Frau was quite capable of handling nasty situations. The Bichon would have Otto as her aide when he returned to Earth. Meanwhile, both Galatea and Chita would be with her. Special Agent Badger would be in the neighborhood. Each psychic would have an Ursula.

The team boarded the Twin Otter for the trip south to New Orleans MSY airport. Ben was staying behind. Look out Gaston, here they come!

*****

Meanwhile, back on planet Orb, the Imperial audience was proceeding. Otto had presented his company, putting special emphasis on the importance of the Bearoness and her consort in Mediana *(Earth)* affairs. The Twins were introduced as the scion and scioness of this noble family and the major reasons for this interplanetary tour. He then acknowledged Howard as both a scientific genius and the facilitator of their journeys. As for himself, the Otter revealed that he would be leaving the group, at least temporarily, as he had been called back to deal with a knotty issue on Mediana.

Emperor Merow expressed his pleasure at being visited by such an outstanding team of visitors and extended the hospitality of his country to them. Magister Purre, who had returned to the Throne Room, would serve as their host while they were in Orient. Merow regretted the forthcoming departure of Magician Otto but looked forward to having talks with the others. Toward that end, he extended an invitation to dinner that evening which the group gratefully accepted.

The Magister then took the opportunity to present the priests and courtiers who were in attendance. One of the priests, a wizened feline with grizzled hair and a rattling voice, pugnaciously asked, "Who are these gods you serve? They who forbid you to tell us how you traveled here. Since our gods are the only true divinities of the universe, you are sinful idolators."

The Emperor pounded his ornate staff on the marble floor in front of his throne. "Enough, Leonidas, I will not have you insulting our visitors."

"You should expel them as the dangerous threats they are. They are here to undermine our sacred beliefs."

The Emperor hissed. "You are a paranoid fanatic. Leave this throne room immediately and stay out of my sight. If I hear you are harassing our guests, it will not go well with you."

The priest snarled and limped from the room. As he left he shook his staff at the travelers.

Merow shook his head. "I apologize for our High Priest. I'll explain further when I see you all this evening at dinner. Magister Purre will show you to your rooms where you can relax after your journey."

The courtier shrugged in dismay and echoed the Merow's apologies. As he led the group through the magnificent halls to the residence wing, he said, "That was just the latest in an ongoing series of disputes between the priests and the Merow. Leonidas would like nothing better than to see the Emperor and his government overthrown and replaced by a Theocratic Council with him at the head. It won't happen, of course. But the Emperor's patience and tolerance of the priests is growing very short. I fear something unpleasant may break out. Hopefully after you have concluded your visit.

Belinda peered at Octavius, Howard and Otto. Concern on her face.

McTavish looked at Arabella, "Oh, Boy! That priest's trouble!"

Chapter Five

On their way to the famous Big Easy
Where the living is fun filled and breezy
It's the Femme Private Eyes
And they plan the demise
Of a drug lord both nasty and sleazy.

The DHC-6-300 Twin Otter requires a fuel stop between Cincinnati and New Orleans. The Wolves were at the controls as they worked their way into the hectic traffic patterns surrounding Hartsfield-Jackson Airport in Atlanta. The Colonel snarled, "This place is an aerial traffic jam. Busy, Busy, Busy!"

The Frau chuckled, "A good place to catch up on approach and departure discipline. Keep calm, Wyatt. They're doing their best and so are we."

Eventually they were cleared for landing, touched down and taxiied the turboprop to the General Aviation sector for refueling. Galatea, another pilot, had been sitting in the cockpit jumpseat observing. She was used to the Concorde and C-5A with their high speed, long range jet characterstics or helicopters. The prop driven Twin Otter was a different kind of flying. "Nice going guys! Now, let's see you get us back out of here."

Chita and Mlle Woof were sitting in the main cabin by themselves. Neither were flight enthusiasts. For safety's sake, they got off the plane during refueling. Giselle had been discussing techniques for her divination act matching Frau Ilse's. Both were skilled actresses but Mlle Woof spoke Parisian French and Frau Schuylkill a Swiss variation. They didn't know what dialect Gaston spoke. Some patois, probably. Unless he absolutely insisted on it, they intended to speak English during their sittings. *(The spirits required it.)* A carefully hidden Ursula would provide disembodied voices.

Assuming Gaston went to both of them, Giselle and Ilse needed to coordinate their performances, suggesting that he was in danger from rivals and could not trust members of his mob. But they had to do it in a way that did not suggest any collusion or communication on their own parts. They had to ignore each other's existence or, if asked, cast unfavorable opinions on their abilities.

They had to wait until they were in their residences to actually rehearse their routines. Neither wanted to use a crystal ball. *"Corny and old-fashioned."* They settled on decks of cards. One Tarot and one deck of standard playing cards. That way, Gaston could shuffle and cut the decks. Otto, a not so hot magician, was nevertheless an expert on handling and dealing cards and was ready to pass on his expertise to the two seers when he arrived.

Galatea called Chita and Giselle back to the Twin Otter. They buttoned up, spun up the props and after getting clearance, taxiied away from the service area and got onto the conga line of aircraft waiting on the taxiways for permission to take to the air. It took a while but finally they were vectored to a short runway and used the STOL features of the Otter to get off and away from the heavies who were on their way to circle the world.

An uneventful run to MSY New Orleans Airport. They had rented two cars to take them to the hotel and condo. The wolves took up residence in the French Quarter Hotel and Chita, Galatea and Mlle Woof occupied the pied-à-terre. When Otto arrived, Galatea would fly the Twin Otter back to the Bear's Lair with a stop this time in far less crowded Nashville. From here on, the two soothsayers could not be seen together in New Orleans. Ursulas would be keeping them informed of what was what with each other.

Special Agent Badger was doing her part. The FBI had an undercover agent in Gaston's gang named Luciano reporting back on the mob's activities. It was his job to bring the two fortune tellers to Gaston's attention.

With their concentration on the druglord, they had neglected to deal with the possibility that others might want their services. Neither of them believed in soothsaying and they were reluctant to scam innocent parties with spiritist nonsense. One of Chita's and Wyatt's assignments was to ward off potential clients except of course, Gaston Le Chien, or anyone from his group. Illness, full schedules, unfavorable positioning of the stars, restless spirits etc. etc. were all to be invoked if an insistent clientele began to appear.

Both Giselle and Frau Ilse went through a series of rehearsals with Chita, Galatea and Wyatt respectively. They made contact with Special Agent Badger, her embedded spy and Miguel, the Mexican Ocelot actor who was to play the part of Gaston's new rival. He was being amply paid for the risk he was taking. The Octavians were getting their usual stipends and support. The process unfolded and Giselle and Galatea waited for Otto's arrival.

*****

Meanwhile, back on Planet Orb, the Otter was preparing for his departure back to Mediana *(Earth)* with a precise vector to New Orleans and Madame Giselle, all under the direction of Marlin and Ursula. The AGI was making full use of her superlative multi-tasking abilities, managing affairs on Orb with Howard including Otto's upcoming Multiverse journey and lending Earthbound support to the anti-drug co-conspirators. In the words of the Colonel, "Busy, busy, busy!"

At the Orient Palace, the space tourists were enjoying a sumptuous meal with the Emperor and Magister Purre. The Twins were awed. Their chambers were the height of luxury. They had been issued resplendent blue and gold robes by way of dinner clothes. Belinda was bedecked in her Bearonial jewels. The food was great and the Twins listened to Merow with rapt attention. Belinda, Octavius, Howard and Otto were similarly enthralled.

"I have been Emperor for fifteen years. My father was Emperor before me. My mother, the Dowager Empress and my wife Empress Catrin will be joining us shortly. We have one daughter, Princess Apricot, who is away at school."

"I have great ambitions for Orient and Orb in its entirety. The Occident, on the other side of the Great Ocean, is small, tribal and nomadic, led by independent chieftains. They have chosen to have little to do with Orient. I am hoping we can change that through commerce and trade. Even nomads have an eye for profit."

"I have no aspirations for conquest. We maintain a small defense force and navy. Orient has thriving marine industries: fishing, shipping, exploring, even tourist and recreation. We have embarked on aviation both commercially and militarily but thus far, it is in its early stages. We have a railroad. Our communications technology is just adequate but I want it to be faster and capable of serving a much wider area of the planet. I have approved major investments in construction, engineering, science and education facilities to support them. I believe I am forward looking. Would you agree, Magister Purre?"

"Oh yes, sire. Perhaps too enlightened for certain factions. "

"Yes, there is that. You saw a demonstration earlier in the day. The High Priest Leonidas and his followers are opposed to what they call sinful ambition in opposition to the will of the gods. They would have us reduced to the same status as the Occident nomads. Sheer nonsense but troublesome nonsense. I have been tempted to banish them but they have a substantial hold on the minds and emotions of some of the people, especially the elderly and poorly educated. My hopes are on the middle class, the military, the young workers and students such as your two youngsters and my daughter. Our schools are improving but not as rapidly as I would like. Ah, here come the Ladies."

The Dowager and the Empress entered, bowed to the sovereign and approached to be kissed. The Empress Mother looked very much like an Earth born lioness of advanced age. The Empress was reminiscent of a mature puma. Both were elegantly attired with a full panoply of precious gems on display. They bowed to the "Medianic" assemblage, casting special attention on the Bearoness. They seated themselves in empty seats to the left and right of the Emperor and two "footcats" served them the first course. *(Thus far, the Emperor and his court seemed to regard Octavius simply as Belinda's consort with no special attributes of his own and Howard, the Porcupine, as the hired help. Magician Otto was the other focus of their attention. The Twins thought this was hilarious but said nothing.)*

The Empress spoke in Belinda's general direction. "We apologize for our late arrival. A little court incident that needed immediate attention." She turned to her husband. "The High Priest again. Berating me about Apricot being away at school. Females should only receive training in the wisdom of the gods. They have no need of secular schooling. He is a superannuated fossil."

44

"But a dangerous fossil, unfortunately, my dear. I was just discussing him with our friends from Mediana. He accused them this morning of coming here to undermine the teachings of our gods. He wants them expelled."

The Dowager smiled and looked at the Bearoness. "Well, are you?"

"Are we what, your Highness?"

"Here to undermine the teachings of our gods. If you are, I will lend you my whole hearted support."

"Now Mother, behave!"

Belinda chuckled, "No Empress. We have no intentions of involving ourselves in Orient's religion."

"A pity. Magician Otto, I understand you are gifted with occult abilities. You must be an irritant to the High Priest."

"My abilities are not occult, Your Highness. No gods or spirits are involved. Just enhanced applied physics and genetics."

"Physics, genetics? Are those sciences? Unfortunately my scientific knowledge is severely limited. My generation is ill equipped to deal with it. That gives the priests their advantage. That is why it is so important that young Orienters such as Apricot be trained in the principles and application of these subjects. Are these Twins of yours so educated, Bearoness?"

"They most definitely are, your highness. My consort, Doctor Octavius Bear, is a renowned scientist and engineer and he has ensured that our offspring are well trained in the various physical disciplines."

Arabella blurted, "We are especially good at computing and electronics."

The Dowager shook her head. "Computing, electronics. More than I can handle. But in spite of the priests, our children should gain these skills. Meantime, let us finish our dinner and perhaps, Magician Otto, you could demonstrate some of your abilities. I understand you will be leaving us shortly."

"Indeed, I will be, Empress, but first let me pour you a glass of wine."

The bottle rose telekinetically, filled her glass and returned to the table.

"Clumsy me! It seems I spilled a bit on the tablecloth." A napkin climbed on its own power and dabbed at a tiny spot of wine. The non-Medianans gaped. Several of the guards gripped their weapons more tightly. One of the serving footcats picked up the bottle and examined it.

"I'm sorry. I did not mean to upset you. Perhaps, it is best if I leave."

Ursula and Howard took the hint and Otto disappeared with a gentle 'whoosh.' The Emperor's wife who had been silent during the demonstration, exclaimed, "How does he do that?"

Octavius chuckled, "Only he knows how."

"Are any of you similarly gifted?"

"Afraid not, Your Highness. It is a most particular talent. Not something one can learn."

Ursula quietly murmured. "Thank goodness."

The evening progressed with a combination of small talk and the Emperor's aspirations for the planet. They paid more attention to Octavius who proved he was not just the lumbering companion of the brilliant Bearoness. His insightful questions and suggestions interested the Emperor and Magister.. They discussed aviation, a favorite of the Emperor's. The Twins had been warned against introducing the concept of the Internet or their games.

Arabella turned to the Empress Catrin and said, 'Please tell us about your daughter, Princess Apricot."

The Empress smiled. "She is a highly intelligent, accomplished and hyperactive young lady. Much like you, I surmise. I'm sorry she is not here to meet you. She would be so excited. We found her a school that is not infected by the superstitious rumblings of Leonidas and his ilk. Merow and I are working diligently to detach him and his priests from Orient's education system. It is essential to achieving the progress we so desire."

Chapter Six

Otto's back from his trip into space
With some aches that he'd like to erase.
He is ready to help!
First a big gulp of kelp
Then he'll bring all his skills to the case.

The New Orleans program was moving on apace when Otto arrived at Giselle Woof's apartment. Chita, Galatea and the Bichon were relaxing with bowls of wine and Scotch.

"Otto! Hello!"

"Greetings, Ladies, Oof! These quantum leaps can be a bit of a strain but here I am, ready to assist. Ursula, would you please let Howard and Octavius know I arrived OK. Chita, a bowl of fermented kelp juice would be very refreshing. Thank you!"

"Relax for few minutes and we'll bring you up to speed."

They outlined the situation, told him about Frau Ilse's location and suggested he could 'zap' invisibly to her hotel suite without arousing suspicion. Between him and Ursula they could coordinate their activities. The She-Wolf and Bichon had developed their stories and techniques independently, keeping the essentials but changing each sufficiently to avoid the appearance of duplication or conspiracy. Giselle would use Tarot cards. Ilse would employ normal playing cards. Otto would teach both of them sleight of hand methods for managing the card decks. It was now up to the FBI's embedded agent to discover the two 'clairvoyants' and pass this information on to Gaston. Miguel, the Ocelot actor playing the Mexican druglord rival was also making himself known.

Special Agent Badger had several of her investigators in town. They were picking off some of Gaston's mob members and shipments and generally harassing his operations. They hoped this would inspire the superstitious dog to seek advice from the two new seers and cause conflict within the gang. They would just have to wait for him to react.

Now that Otto had arrived, Galatea planned to fly the Twin Otter back to Cincinnati in the morning. She and Ben would stand by at the Bear's Lair to pick them all up again at the end of the sting.

Chita queried Ursula, "What can you tell us about Gaston?

The AGI responded. "We don't know if or when to expect a visit from him. Superstitious as he's supposed to be, I don't imagine he'll want to pass up an opportunity to get more guidance from the spirits. Not sure what his reaction will be to bad news, however. He's hot headed but not stupid. He couldn't head up a money-making enterprise if he was a complete dope. *(No pun intended)* Unlike other members of his gentle breed, he's said to have a fierce, hair-trigger temper. He has killed off rivals, traitors and failures."

Mlle Woof snuffled. "Do you think Frau Ilse and I will be in danger? Will he shoot the messenger?"

"I don't think so. He'd be afraid of supernatural revenge. Otto, Chita and I will be standing by, however. He may try to shut you down and force you out of the city."

"That's OK by me."

"Yes, that would trigger your escape. I'm going to have a session with Frau Schuylkill now. Otto, why don't you 'zap' over to her hotel? I'm on her laptop, too. I have to prepare my 'disembodied' voice for you all to use."

The Frau and Colonel were none too successfully attempting to manipulate a deck of 52 standard playing cards along with Ursula when Otto landed in their midst.

"Hi, folks. Just got back from outer space and boy, are my arms tired. OK, the joke is tired. The exoplanet Orb. Interesting place and beings. After I 'zapped' around and moved a few items telekinetically, I had them believing I was a magician. Our tourists are being regaled by the Emperor and his court. One fly in the ointment. The High Priest wants them gone. He believes they are there to undermine their religion. Ursula is keeping track. Howard, Octavius and Belinda are all ready to deal with him if he acts up. As is the Emperor."

"Now, to businss here. Let's see. You will be using a standard fifty-four card deck with the usual four suits and two jokers. Leave the jokers in. Shuffle and cut the deck and pick a card, any card! Ta-da! A joker. Let's try again. Shuffle, cut. Another joker! OK ditch the two jokers We're going to want to bring up the Ace of Spades. Shuffle again. This time cut twice and shuffle one more time. Pick your card. Ace of Spades! Let me show you how it was done. I was a lousy magician but a pretty good card sharp."

"Mlle Woof, sorry, Giselle, is working on the Tarot deck along with Chita. She needs to learn how to bring up the right cards, too. Between the two of you, we'll get Gaston shook up if the FBI hasn't done that already. I'll get you guys started and go back to her. Oh, boy! What fun! 'Zapping' around the Big Easy!" He landed back in the apartment in time to see the Bichon spread a five card array. All foretelling dire results.

"Not bad, Mamselle. You'll be in great demand with the tourists when you get back to Polar Paradise. 'Appearing tonight. Giselle the Tarot Queen.' Only you'll have to work up some jolly predictions. Keep the vacationing Polars in good spirits. Ha! Your French accent is getting more pronounced. *(Puns intended.)* Chita, you look positively exotic but then you always do."

"Madame Catt to you, Otter. I am practicing my mysterious feline act to support Madame Giselle. Her puppy-cut curly white fur, pert black nose and soulful eyes are perfect to disguise her as a talented but innocent student of the mystic arts. She is sooo believable. I, on the other hand, am shadowy and enigmatic adding just a touch of discomfort to the atmosphere. You know, you're right. We ought to take this show on the road. Frau Schuylkill and Wyatt are scary and baffling as wolves should be. What a combination."

The Otter chuckled. "I'll have to chat with Talent Agent Maury when I get back. Mlle Woof has been searching for a replacement gig now that the Twins have grown up. She'd be a natural at the Shetlands resort. Combine her with an all knowing Ursula and the fun would be outstanding. Maybe we could talk the Wolves into making guest appearances. And you, show girl that you are, would be tremendous. I could do a little magic just to add to the routine. I started out as a magician. Ended up as a clown."

The Development of Civilization Volume 17
Part 3
Cartomancy - The Tarot
From "An Introduction to Faunapology"

by Octavius Bear Ph.D.

Cartomancy is fortune-telling or divination using a special deck of cards. It arose in Paris during the 1780s, using the Tarot of Marseilles. The Marseilles pattern is highly popular today.

Cartomancers tell us that the entire universe exists within a Tarot deck, with each card representing a person, place, or event. The 78-card Tarot deck used by esotericists has two distinct parts.

The Major Arcana cards, which speak of greater secrets, and the Minor Arcana cards, which involve lesser mysteries.

The Major Arcana or trumps, consists of 22 cards without suits:

The Magician, The High Priestess, The Empress, The Emperor, The Hierophant, The Lovers, The Chariot, Strength, The Hermit, Wheel of Fortune, Death, Justice, The Hanged Man, Temperance, The Devil, The Tower, The Star, The Moon, The Sun, Judgement, The World and The Fool.

Cards from The Magician to The World are numbered in Roman numerals from I to XXI, while The Fool is the only unnumbered card, sometimes placed at the beginning of the deck as 0, or at the end as XXII.

The Minor Arcana has 56 cards, divided into four suits of 14 each. Ten numbered cards and four court cards. The court cards are the King, Queen, Knight and Page/Jack, in each of the four Tarot suits. The traditional Tarot suits are swords, batons, coins and cups. In modern occult Tarot decks, the batons suit is often called wands, rods or staves, while the coins suit is often called pentacles or disks

The Major Arcana cards represent monumental, groundbreaking influences. Each stands alone as a powerful message, representing life-changing motions that define the beginnings or ends of cycles. These dynamic cards appear during major transitions, signaling distinctive moments of transformation. The cards are numbered to represent stations within our greater journey through life; their chronological order reveals the passing of time.

The Minor Arcana cards, on the other hand, reflect everyday matters. The Minor Arcana cards are broken up into four suits, each containing ten numbered cards and four court cards. In the Minor Arcana, the card's number reveals the stage of an event: The ace card represents the beginning, while the 10 symbolizes the end.

Similarly, the progression of the court cards demonstrates our understanding of circumstances on an individual level, representing either personality types or actual people.

The Page (or Princess, in some decks), Knight, Queen, and King interpret circumstances with increasing levels of understanding and wisdom.

The suits (Wands, Pentacles, Swords, and Cups) correspond to their own unique areas of life and astrological elements. Wands symbolize passion and inspiration (the fire element). Pentacles represent money and physical realities (the earth element). Swords depict intellectual intrigues (the air element), and Cups illustrate emotional matters (the water element). These suits reveal which spheres of influence are being activated.

There are a variety of spreads used by different practitioners. One card, three card, five card. One card is often good for a yes or no answer while a more complex five card spread can be much more informative. The position of the card, upright or reversed, indicates a different message.

The querent may shuffle and cut the deck and select the cards. But, in the last analysis, it is up to the medium to create the spread and interpret meaning. Therein lies the art of cartomancy.

Our two practitioners of divination are learning the techniques of predicting from the Tarot and the standard playing card deck. Their skills will be enhanced by Ursula 14 and her Augmented Reality capabilities. Stay tuned.

Chapter Seven

The fanatics come after the Twins.
They believe they are guilty of sins.
One attacks with a staff.
It's a serious gaffe.
And he ends up with welts on his shins.

Meanwhile, back on Orb, dinner had concluded and the tour group was escorted into a splendid library where post prandial drinks awaited. The Twins decided they wanted to go exploring and the Emperor assigned two guards to accompany them. They left the Palace and spied an impressive structure nearby towering in a grove of trees. Arabella asked the guard, Simon, what it was.

"That is the Supreme Temple where the gods of Orient are worshipped. It is also the home of Leonidas, the High Priest and several of his ministers and acolytes. There are temples scattered about Orient and a few on Occident but this is the religious center of the planet."

"Is it permitted to enter?"

Simon replied "I'm not sure, young bear. It is open to all of the Orient faithful but I do not know how someone from off-planet would be welcomed. I was there this morning when Leonidas shook his staff at you and told the Emperor to have you expelled."

"Well," said McTavish, "We don't want to cause any trouble. Let's just get a closer look but not go in."

Too late. Out of one of the Temple's doors came a crowd of white robed cats, brandishing staffs and yowlng. Leonidas was in the vanguard.

"Idolators. How dare you soil the sacred sanctum with your unworthy feet. You and your pagan scum family will be driven from our shores. The Emperor will not be able to help you."

One of the disciples, no doubt trying to impress the High Priest, ran up and took a swipe at Arabella with his staff. The guard standing next to her slammed the acolyte's legs with his spear. He dropped his staff and ran back to his cronies, shrieking in pain. Before Leonidas could get another word in, the guard shouted. "How dare you attack the honored guests of the Emperor. I know you, Jasper. You shall be reported to His Majesty and you too, High Priest. Shame on you all."

They returned to the Imperial Palace where Simon reported to Magister Purre. He, in turn, approached the Emperor. "Sire, Jasper, one of Leonidas' acolytes attacked the young bears. Simon warded him off. "

"Well done, Simon. Have Jasper imprisoned and summon Leonidas to me. This is a disgrace. Bearoness, Doctor Bear, young Twins, Doctor Watt. You have my most sincere apologies. Such behavior will not be tolerated in my realm."

Arabella snuffled, "Oh, that's OK, your majesty…"

"No, it is not, young lady. The High Priest and his minions have grown increasingly arrogant and fanatic. They would like nothing better than to overthrow me and set up a theocracy. They have twisted the personalities of the gods in the minds of the people. Where once they were benevolent entities, they are now vengeful and fearsome. The Priests believe they themselves are untouchable. I shall disabuse them of that illusion, starting with Leonidas."

Belinda looked at her team and then the Emperor. "Your Majesty, it seems our presence here is causing strife. We do not wish to create any more animosity between you and the Priests. I believe it would be in everyone's interest for us to depart and return to our home in Mediana."

Octavius nodded his head in agreement. "Your Majesty, it is best if we do not get involved in the internal issues of your realm. I agree with my consort. I'm sure our children are also reluctant to be the unwitting triggers of conflict between the Priests and your noble self. It would seem you have sufficient grievances against them without our adding to the list. We most sincerely thank you for your wonderful hospitality and let me say on behalf of all of us, we are most impressed with you and your domain. Please extend our very best wishes to your wife and the Dowager Empress. Our thanks to you too, Magister Purre and to you, Simon, for protecting our daughter."

The Emperor frowned but acquiesced. "Go with my blessing. Your departure will not alter my plans for Leonidas, however. His comeuppance is long overdue. We have enjoyed your presence. Travel safely."

They returned to their quarters. Howard activated their quantum jump.

*****

Safely back at the Bear's Lair, the space tourists were recovering and regrouping from their Multiverse trip. Huntley was on deck with refreshments and blankets. Space travel can be cold. Even a short journey from a parallel universe. The twins were disappointed at the need for an early exit.

McTavish grunted. "Those priests were a bunch of thugs. And Leonidas was the Chief Thug."

Octavius agreed. "Right, son, but if there was going to be a religious civil war, we couldn't be a part of it. When Otto gets back from New Orleans, we'll send him on a short reconnaissance jaunt to Orb to see what, if anything, happened. Meanwhile, let's see of if we can come up with a good next alternative. Your mother is set on exploring the cosmos and I'm sure you two want to as well. What do you think, Howard? Can you and Marlin come up with another destination?"

"I'm sure we can, Octavius. Give us a day or so to investigate and set up something. It would help to have Otto act as a scout but he's tied up for the moment."

*****

Indeed he was. He was showing the Frau and Colonel the techniques and intricacies of card manipulation, sleight of hand, artifice and ruse. While he was demonstrating lifts, false deals, side steals, passes, palming, false shuffles, false cuts, color changes, crimps, jogs, reverses and forces, the two wolves looked on in amazement.

"Otto, we'll never be able to master all of that or any of that."

"I know. I'm just showing off. There is one trick I want you to learn, though. It's called the Ambitious Card. You make it show up pretty much on command even after cutting and shuffling the deck. In Gaston's case, you want the Spades suit – Ace, King and eight, all foretelling misfortune, betrayal and rivalry and the four and eight of Clubs saying essentially the same thing. Gaston will probably recognize them for what they are. Make sure he cuts and shuffles the deck. Don't bring out all of those cards on the first passes. If he insists on recutting and shuffling, bring up each one separately. We want him worried and vindictive. Now let me show you how to make a card ambitious."

They went through the exercises and lo and behold, the Ace of Spades surfaced on the first pass, then the King and finally the eight. Each time Wyatt, pretending to be Gaston, cut the deck and Ilse brought up the ambitious card.

"OK, let's bring up the four and eight of clubs. Same results. Now, we have to concoct a story. He's probably familiar with the meaning of the cards that are appearing. Keep your comments low key and only make suggestions if he doesn't react. Let him draw his own conclusions."

"If he gets violent, you two know how to deal with him. Wyatt, make sure he isn't packing a weapon. If he is, refuse to let him in. If he insists, I'll get involved and toss him telekinetically. I'll be hiding with Ursula. He'll probably have one of his goons with him. On the other hand, it may be Luciano, Special Agent Badger's spy. We'll just have to see. Under no circumstances, agree to come to him. He has to come to you. He won't want to but his inquisitiveness will finally do him in. Cats aren't the only ones who succumb to curiosity. OK, we wait and you keep practicing."

"I'm on my way back to Giselle and Chita. They're making great progress and Mlle Woof has her accent and all her theatrical tricks up to full speed. I think she's on her way to a new career. We should consider making this into a movie or at least a TV serial."

Wyatt and Ilse waved at him as he once more 'zapped.' She laughed. "He makes himself out to be hopeless goofball but there goes one of the sharpest members of the Octavian team. Gaston doesn't stand a chance."

Chapter Eight

The Great Pyrenees Dog was upset.
He saw all of his gang as a threat.
A new rival in town.
His receipts were all down.
With an even worse case coming yet.

Gaston was his usual nervous self, snarling at his associates and barking at the slightest upset. His drug running enterprises were being harassed by the Feds and he had heard that a new rival was in town – Miguel, a Mexican Ocelot, if you could believe it. Like most dogs, he hated cats, especially cats who were intent on moving into his business and territory. No way that was going down. The Great Pyrenees mockingly referred to him as El Raton Miguelito-Mickey Mouse.

"Luciano, what's happening?" *(Luciano, a Huge Neapolitan Mastiff, was the FBI's embedded spy.)*

"Bad news and good news, Boss. The Feds hit another one of our shipments."

"Someone is giving them advance notice. I want that traitor found and disposed of."

"Si, Si! We are on it. I'm creating a phony consignment and only telling a couple of the boys. If the Feds go after it we've narrowed down the bad eggs."

"See to it. What's your good news?"

"There are a couple of famous new fortune tellers in town. I know how much you believe in that spiritualist and divination stuff. Two females. A wolf and a dog. They're rivals. They hate one another. One is on a tour and the other has taken an apartment in the Warehouse District and is moving in. They do card readings. Tarot, whatever that is, and regular cards."

"Good. No crystal balls, palmistry or seances. Can't stand those fake theatrics. Find them and bring them here."

"They may insist on you coming to them."

"Nobody insists on Gaston coming to them."

*****

Mlle Giselle Woof had just finished two mock sessions with Chita going through the Tarot cards and interpreting the bad news they foretold. Otto arrived just in time to assist.

"Hi, Ladies! I just had another session with the Wolves. They're coming along nicely with the standard deck. How are you doing on Tarot?"

"We decided we need to have a fairly consistent showing of Major Arcana cards. Not all, mind you. Too obvious, but a few signaling hard times and serious problems. Enough to make him believe he is being betrayed."

"Here they are: the Tower - disaster! The Moon Reversed - confusion and fear! The Star Reversed - faithlessness! Death - end of cycle! Chariot Reversed - loss of control! The Magician - Trickery! In the Minor Arcana – Pentacles - money and finances! Now, we have to figure out how to make them appear in several five card spreads mixed with a few harmless items."

"OK, a little sleight of hand and false deals along with false cuts and shuffles and we should be able to make them show as you want."

Chita chirped, "But he's going to cut and shuffle."

"That's what you want him to think. That's where the sleight of hand comes in. Here, let me show you."

And so it went. The Bichon's paws getting more and more facile as she repeated and repeated the motions. She delivered the identity of the cards and their meaning in a low French accent. No small talk. Just a flat, unemotional recitation. She issued the warnings in a matter of fact way, occasionally looking up at Chita who was playing the part of Gaston.

Otto clapped, "OK, time to get Gaston set up. I'll contact Luciano. I think the Pyrenees will want you to come to him. We'll have to convince him that's not good idea. I'll have to do a little stealthy 'zapping' and with some help from Ursula, have the sprits summon him to your presence. For all of his deadly command and control, at bottom, he's a superstitious jerk."

57

Chapter Nine

A return to the Earth and Bear's Lair.
To decide on their next trip to where?
Off to Rhea and then
Gaea's Homo Sap men?
That's a species that's terribly rare.

Back at the Bear's Lair, the travelers were finishing off a hearty brunch. Howard had gone down to the Multiverse lab to confer with Marlin and check in with Ursula.

"Where's Otto? How is he doing?"

Ursula replied. "He's in New Orleans with the fake cartomancers getting them ready to upset Gaston's applecart. Galatea is flying to the Bear's Lair in the Twin Otter this morning. She and Ben will be standing by to hurry back to pick up the Wolves, Madame Woof and Chita when the divination sessions are over. Otto will either join them or 'zap' back on his own power."

"Good! Octavius and I would like him to take another blitz trip back to Orb to see what, if anything, is happening with the Emperor and the High Priest. That could be trouble. Meanwhile, our alternate universe tourists are eager to see another world since this trip was cut short. Marlin, what have we got for them?"

The Dolphin squeaked and splashed in his ample tank. "Should we send them to Gaea and let them meet up with Homo Sapiens? The Twins would be enthralled. Gaea has moved along quite smartly in developing technology and social order. Of course, they've had clandestine animal representatives here on Earth for quite a while. Remember Winnipeg and the Opera Director. *(See Book 4 – The Lower Case)* No H. Saps came over. They would have stuck out on our all-animal planet. What do you think?"

Howard scrunched up his porcupine nose. "Maybe we should send them to Rhea, too. *(See Book 14 – The Nut Case)* That crazy Admiral is dead and his Company is disbanded. The Council and Triumvirate have been shuffled. Priscilla Porcupine's Uncle Portnoy is once again the Chief

Executive Chairbeast. Any interplanetary invasion plans the Admiral was advocating and developing have been scrapped. Octavius, Belinda and I can verify the situation and Otto can join us when he wraps up in New Orleans."

The Dolphin laughed, "That's two trips for Otto. Octavius wants him to go back to Orb and check on the Emperor/High Priest conflict. Of course, on Rhea, you'll get another chance to see the attractive and elusive Priscilla. She's probably still in the market for a Chief Science Officer plus."

Marlin laughed again. It's tough to tell with his spiny face but Howard was blushing. "Let's talk to Octavius and Belinda."

*****

Howard found Octavius and Belinda in the Lair's Lounge. The Twins were sitting with their laptops checking on the progress of their Internet game - The Bold Brave Brilliant Bumptious Bears. While they went touring Australia and the universe, they had turned its development and distribution over to a group of gamester geeks at the Deep Data Hexagon. It was going gangbusters with new characters and plot situations. The Twins were of two minds on the subject. While they were pleased that the game was doing so well, they also missed the fun of working on it and signing up new players. But they did want to see more of the cosmos. The prospect of meeting new species, especially H. Saps, fascinated them.

The Porcupine scientist presented the two choices. Gaea or Rhea. The Twins immediately jumped on the bandwagon. "Why not both?" Belinda considered the options. She knew Octavius wasn't crazy about Gaea. A couple of bad incidents but the exoplanet was quite similar to Earth with H. Saps and that might appeal to the Twins. Rhea was different in many ways but similar enough not to be outlandish. She looked at Octavius. "We could do both. We're somewhat familiar with Gaea but the Twins and I know nothing about Rhea. Tell us, Howard."

The Porcupine snuffled, "Alright, Rhea in a nutshell: The planet has seven geographic city-states. The largest is called Prime City. It's the seat of planetary government. Home of the Governing Council. Each city-state has an elected representative on the Council. A triumvirate is a sort of steering committee. All told, there are fifteen Council members, all males. Most, but not all are equine. In addition to the seven city-state representatives, eight more are functional specialists - finance; defense; health and welfare; security and justice; science and education; transport; agriculture; business. The Triumvirate is in overall charge. The Council Chairbeast, who is the real Chief Executive, rotates every three years among the city-state members. The head of the Science Center is Priscilla Porcupine. The current Council member for Prime City is Priscilla's Uncle Portnoy. Another Porcupine. He is the Chairbeast and quite influential. I'm sure she and he would make us welcome after the near-miss episode with Admiral Tumult."

Arabella squeaked. "Let's go to Rhea first and stop at Gaea on the way back. I want to meet an H.Sap." McTavish agreed. Octavius looked at Bel, shrugged his massive shoulders and said to Howard. "OK, make it so. Ursula, what do you think?

The AGI paused and then said, "I think it will work out well. I'm not sure what is going to happen in New Orleans but we have more than enough talent assigned to that process including Otto. He's quite a card sharp."

Octavius grinned, "Get a hold of Otto and tell him what we have in mind. See what he thinks and then let's set up a two planet voyage. Day after tomorrow if Otto doesn't have any problems. Let Senhor Condor know our plans. Check and see if the Flying Tigers want to come along. They didn't make the trip to Orb."

The Twins did a high five. Belinda chuckled and Howard turned to go down to the Multiverse Lab to work things out with Marlin. Huntley came into the lounge and refilled their drink bowls. "Will you be traveling again, Sir and Madame? I'll prepare a light set of luggage for each one of you, if you are. What will the weather be like?"

Belinda scratched her nose. "I honestly don't know, Huntley. Howard and Otto will be able to tell you. Thank you for your assistance. Sorry we have to leave you here but someone has to manage the Lair."

"And that's what you hired me to do, Bearoness. Besides, I'm not all that enthused about interplanetary trekking."

Arabella had the last word, "But we are, Huntley. We are!"

Chapter Ten

Gaston's aggravated and how.
There are problems he just can't allow.
He dislikes what he hears.
He will summon the seers.
He wants all the answers and now!

The Great Pyrenees Mountain Dog rustled in his bed struggling with a disturbed sleep. He kept hearing voices speaking to him in Louisiana French, the language of most Cajuns and Creoles. Gaston was a European bilingual, speaking a heavily dialected English combined with French/Spanglish. He understood the voices and growled in return.

The sounds emanated from a small device carefully concealed under the dog's bed chamber furniture by Luciano, the FBI operative. The female voice was one of Ursula's almost infinite number.

She whispered that he was the victim of conspirators and traitors who were seeking to take over his establishment and lucrative trade. Miguel, the Mexican Ocelot, was preparing to move in on him with the help of the turncoats in his gang.

A half-awake Gaston snarled at the prospect. The subtle voice suggested he seek further guidance from two females skilled at divination – one French, the other Swiss, newly arrived in the Big Easy. The dog blinked. Luciano had said something about new clairvoyants in town. He'll have the Mastiff bring them to him. He trusted Luciano up to a point. Gaston's paranoia and superstition were extreme. 'Distrust most and rely on the spirits.' He believed it was what kept him successful and in control. He sat up, yawned and called for his assistant. "Get me those fortune tellers."

"OK, Boss. I don't think they get along. You'll have to work with each one separately."

"That's better. There'll be less chance of them conniving against me. I'm getting washed. Bring my breakfast."

He got up and left the room. Luciano waited a few moments and then reached down and removed the small portable transceiver that had been the spirit's *(Ursula)* voice. Breakfast time and then off to see the wizardesses.

*****

"Go back and tell him I do not come to any of my clients. They come to me. The spirits will not commune with me in a foreign environment. It has taken me weeks to establish the proper psychic ambience in this hotel. I will not have it destroyed to accommodate a drug lord."

Frau Schuylkill winked and Luciano chuckled. "He won't be happy."

"Good!"

*****

"Non, non, non. C'est impossible. Madame Giselle does not travel and meet like a penniless gypsy. If M'sieur Gaston wants to avail himself of my formidable services, he must come to me as a humble supplicant seeking enlightenment. There is no alternative. Tell him so."

Chita, Giselle Woof and Luciano all broke into laughter. The Mastiff had his work cut out for him. He went back and reported.

"They said what?"

"They said you must come to them. Each one thinks you are seeking them out alone. They do not know you want to consult their rival as well."

"Tell them to go to Hell. I will not be held off by mystical harpies."

"OK, but you may be missing out on some important advice."

"I don't care. No one gives Gaston orders. I give the commands."

"Fine. I'll just telephone and say, 'Thanks but no thanks!' "

A pawse. "Wait. Which one speaks French?"

"They both do. One's Parisian. She's a Bichon Frisé. The other is Swiss. She's a Grey Wolf."

"Let's use the Bichon first. I prefer white dogs like me. Call her. I'll come but at my convenience. You come, too, with the usual armament."

62

Chapter Eleven

Preparations are running apace
For our travelers' jaunts back to space.
Rhea - first port of call
Then their second landfall
Will be Gaea, a quite Earthlike place

Back at the Bear's Lair, the multiverse travelers were putting the final touches on their travel gear and snarfing down yet another fine breakfast prepared by Huntley. Not in the cordon bleu category of Frau Schuylkill but it would serve well enough. They wondered how she was doing in New Orleans along with Mlle Giselle.

The Flying Tigers had decided to come along on the cosmic journey after they ferried the New Orleans conspirators back to the Bear's Lair. Although they had flown just about every class of aircraft *(except perhaps the Wright Flyer)* interplanetary travel was a new experience for them. Marlin tested them and it turned out they were Multiverse Adepts. They could travel at will and on their own schedule. That made things easier for the entire team – Octavius, Belinda, Howard, the Twins and the Tigers. Otto agreed on the trip to Rhea and would eventually catch up with them after his stint in the Big Easy and a stopover at Orb to get updated on the Emperor/High Priest conflict.

Howard was giving the Twins and Belinda a short briefing on Rhea. "Otto should really be doing this. He was the prime mover *(no pun)* in getting rid of the Admiral and dismantling his Company. As you know, Rhea is a small exoplanet in the Alpha Centauri system and is tight for space. The Admiral was hatching a massive plan for conquering Earth, Gaea or some other planet to provide living room. Now the Rhean Science Center is engaged in looking for uninhabited but habitable planets to peacefully colonize. We don't know what progress they've made. I think I told you, the Center is under the direction of Priscilla Porcupine, the niece of the Council Chairbeast. *(He neglected to mention there was a mild romantic interest between Priscilla and Howard.)* We should be welcomed there."

"I've called up Byzantia Bonobo to give you a rundown on Gaea. As you may know, she worked at the Gaean Telecommunications and Computing Center after she fled Earth. She's back here at the Hex working for Condo on developing Ursula 14 after stopping Caleb Cassowary from destroying our GPS systems in space."

A simian face appeared on the large conference room screen. "Hello, everyone. Byzz Bonobo here. Hi Howard! Greetings Bearoness! Octavius isn't with you, is he? I don't think I've ever met you Twins."

McTavish gave her a virtual high five. "Hi Byzz! I'm McTavish! How are things at the Hex? The geek team is going great with our Bold Brave Brilliant Bumptious Bears game."

"Yes, and I'm using the game to help develop Ursula 14. She's almost ready for Prime Time. Augmented Reality! I'm going to join her with Ursula 13 on one of your next adventures. You must be Arabella. I've heard so much about the two of you."

"Hi Byzz. We've heard about you too. Nice to finally meet you."

"Are the Flying Tigers going with you to Rhea and Gaea?"

"They have a pickup to do in New Orleans and then they'll be joining us, probably on Gaea. Tell us about your experiences there."

"Well, I'm not proud of what I was doing with Caleb here on Earth. By the way, Condo is a real breath of fresh air. Brilliant, energetic, honest and kind. What a difference! Anyway, to escape arrest, we both quantum traveled. I landed on Gaea and he went on to Biosphere X. I think you know the story of how I stopped him from destroying Earth's GPS system."

Belinda replied. "Yes! I gather his cadaver is still floating in planetary orbit. Talk about space junk."

"Yes, well, I'd like to forget that, if I can. Condo and Octavius trust me and I'm having a ball improving the Ursulas. Ursula 14 will have Virtual and Augmented Reality capabilities."

"What about Gaea?"

"There are several different worlds in the cosmos where Homo Sapiens still survives and lives in cooperation with intelligent animals. Gaea is one of them. Octavius discovered that there were about fifty or so Gaeans in small groups around our Earth. *(See Book 4 – The Lower Case)* They seem to be observers and data gatherers. As far as we know, they have not made overt moves, positive or negative toward our planet although they have made efforts to keep their presence a secret. Obviously, the H. Saps can't come to Earth. They'd be immediately recognized. But Gaean sentient animals can and do. Case in point, Dr. Woodrow Wolverine former Director of the Winnipeg Opera. He disappeared along with a Grizzly named Gregory Grigor after the murder of a heifer and arctic fox who were about to reveal the number and locations of the Gaean observers. They went to great lengths to protect their anonymity."

Octavius had arrived and was listening in to Byzz' narration. "Howard, I'm of two minds on this visit to Gaea. It's an exoplanet very similar to ours with the great exception that H. Saps are living there. They know that we are aware of them and of course, their observer teams have been reporting back on us for quite some time. Do they know we have made visitations there in the past?"

Byzz intervened. "I traveled to Gaea several times with a chimpanzee named Joel and made no secret of the fact I was from Earth. There were no repercussions. Then after the Caleb incident here at UUI, I went to work at their Telecom and Computing Center. They knew I was from Earth and still trusted me to work in their satellite program. They're secretive, especially about their ventures to alternate universes but they're not hostile."

The Great Bear nodded and then asked. "Who do we have to contact to get permission to enter their world?"

She replied, "I've been keeping up my relations with my former co-workers and management at the Center. I'll get the Director, who oddly enough is a bear, to arrange clearances, a welcoming committee and all that jazz. I'll make sure you meet a couple of H. Saps. They're very interesting. You can make your journey to Rhea and I'll get everything set up on Gaea and forward the information to you through Ursula."

"By the way, I'm working with some of the Hex technicians to have the Ursulas support you using Augmented Reality. That's part of the Ursula 14 upgrade. You'll get enhanced perception of the environment in which you find yourselves, faster access to information and less need to ask questions. The headsets are either contact lenses or normal fitting eyeglasses, not the big clunky helmets you used to have to wear for virtual reality."

Arabella and McTavish jumped up and down. "That will make our games much more exciting, too. That's great Byzz! Off to the Multiverse."

Howard looked at Belinda and Octavius. They smiled. "OK, first thing in the morning."

Byzantia signed off and Octavius called Howard over. "Do you think our cartomancers in New Orleans could use Augmented Reality headsets?"

"Possibly. Let me talk to Byzz and then I'll call Otto and see what he thinks. If the sets are available, I guess we could get the Tigers to fly down early and deliver them. I'll get right back to you."

Belinda looked at her consort. "I wonder how they're doing down there. I don't like the idea of them being involved with drug dealers."

"They've been involved in dangerous situations before."

"Mlle Woof hasn't."

"She's a big girl, a skilled actress, smart as the proverbial whip and she has Otto and Chita there along with Ursula. And Special Agent Badger has her Mastiff spy there as well. The Wolves can take care of themselves. And Otto will be with them too with an Ursula. I'm betting on them,"

"But Gaston's an impulsive nut. You never know what he'll do."

"What we want him to do is set off a replay of the Valentine's Day massacre. Hopefully on his own gang."

She sighed, "I'm not happy with us causing bloodshed."

"I don't think the FBI will let it get to that. They're ready to pull him in the minute he goes ballistic."

"I hope so. I guess I better get ready for our quantum jumps."

Chapter Twelve

Just a little more practice and then
Our Giselle is all ready for when
Gaston will arrive.
Then she'll smoothly contrive
To deceive him again and again.

In a hushed and darkened apartment in the artsy Warehouse District in downtown New Orleans, Madame Giselle *(Mlle Woof)* and her partner Madame Catt *(Chita)* had just completed another round of practice Tarot readings with Otto and Ursula observing. Chita was playing the part of Gaston, the drug lord, inspecting and shuffling the deck and cutting the cards. Giselle managed a five card spread showing four calamity cards and one benign image.

The Otter applauded. "Congrats. I think you've got it. That was an excellent fake deal. Now all we have to do is wait for Gaston to make an appearance. When is he due?"

Chita responded. "In fifteen minutes, as a matter of fact. If you and Ursula are going to do your thing, you'd better get ready."

They moved the surround sound transceiver device to an ornate mirror that hung in the sitting room. It would transmit Ursula's spirit voice and also record the session. In the center was the divination table covered with a purple velvet cloth under a dimmed small chandelier. It held nothing but the Tarot deck. A second deck was stacked on a small nearby stand in case Gaston insisted on a new series. Three chairs surrounded the table. Otto was hidden in an armoire ready to use his telekinetic powers as needed.

Right on time, the buzzer to the suite sounded and Chita went to answer it. "Good day, gentle beasts! Welcome! Monsieur Luciano, we have met before and this must be Monsieur Gaston Le Chien, our seeker of enlightenment. I am Madame Catt, Madame Giselle's assistant and familiar. Come with me please and I shall introduce you to Madame."

They moved down a dimly-lit corridor toward the large sitting room and there was a sudden metallic clatter on the tiled floor. Two pistols had fallen on top of each other along with a formidable looking cosh. *(Otto's telekinesis at work!)* Gaston and Luciano both stared down at the errant weapons in complete befuddlement.

Chita was her usual sultry self. "Oh, gentlebeasts, naughty, naughty! The spirits will not permit weaponry in their presence. Why don't we just put them on this sideboard here and you may collect them when you leave."

Gaston was gobsmacked. "How did you do that, lady? Hold on! I don't go anywhere without carrying."

"I did nothing, Monsieur. You may address your complaints to the spirits who watch over Madame Giselle and myself."

"I'm not going in there without my pistol."

"Well then. I suppose we must cancel our session. Madame Giselle will be most disappointed. You will still be expected to pay for her services, however. The spirits will demand it."

Luciano, equally flustered but intent on getting Gaston in front of the cartomancer, intervened. "I don't get it, Boss! I've never seen that before. Spooky! She may be the real McCoy if she can conjure up that kind of protection. Maybe we should meet her."

The Great Pyrenees was torn. He believed he was in the presence of some unnatural forces but he was reluctant to let down his guard. Finally his curiosity and superstitious nature overcame his caution. *(cowardice?)* "OK, let's get this going."

Chita looked down her feline nose and said, "Excellent, please come in and be seated. Monsieur Luciano, would be please take that chair by the wall. Monsieur Gaston, please be seated at the table. Madame Giselle, this is Monsieur Gaston Le Chien and his associate Monsieur Luciano. Monsieur Gaston is here seeking your guidance."

Giselle extended her bejeweled paw. "Bon jour, M'sieur. Bienvenu a notre maison. Les esprits sont ici."

The drug lord looked at the curly haired Bichon and said "Let's do this in English, lady. I want my associate to hear and understand what you're saying. "

"Mais certainment, M'sieur. D'accord! Sorry, OK! The Tarot can tell you many things. What answers are your seeking?"

"My business has suddenly turned sour and I want to know why and who is responsible."

"What business is that, Monsieur?"

"You don't have to know that. Let's just say I'm engaged in making animals happy."

"We are the souls of discretion here but if you choose to be secretive, C'est ça. We shall see what the Tarot and the spirits have to say. Are you familiar with the Tarot deck?"

"I've seen them."

She continued. "I use a hybrid of the Ryder-Waite and Marseilles deck of my own invention. The entire universe exists within a Tarot deck, with each card representing a person, place, or event. The 78-card Tarot deck used by us esotericists has two distinct parts."

The Major Arcana cards, which speak to greater secrets, and the Minor Arcana cards, which speak to lesser mysteries.

"The Major Arcana or trump cards, consists of 22 cards:

The Magician, The High Priestess, The Empress, The Emperor, The Hierophant, The Lovers, The Chariot, Strength, The Hermit, Wheel of Fortune, Death, Justice, The Hanged Man, Temperance, The Devil, The Tower, The Star, The Moon, The Sun, Judgement, The World and The Fool."

"Is that clear?"

"Yeah, sort of!"

"Bon! The Minor Arcana consists of 56 cards, divided into four suits of 14 cards each. Ten numbered cards and four court cards. The court cards are the King, Queen, Knight and Page/Jack, in each of the four Tarot suits. The traditional Tarot suits are swords, batons, coins and cups; in my Tarot decks, the batons suit is called wands, while the coins suit is called pentacles. Understood?"

"Yeah! Go on. Let's get to it"

"The Major Arcana cards represent monumental, groundbreaking influences. Each stands alone as a powerful message, representing life-changing motions that define the beginnings or ends of cycles."

"The Minor Arcana cards, on the other hand, reflect everyday matters. The Minor Arcana cards are broken up into four suits, each containing ten numbered cards and four court cards. In the Minor Arcana, the card's number reveals the stage of an event: The ace card represents the beginning, while the 10 symbolizes the end."

"Similarly, the progression of the court cards demonstrates our understanding of circumstances on an individual level, representing either personality types or actual people."

"The Page (or Princess, in my decks), Knight, Queen, and King interpret circumstances with increasing levels of understanding and wisdom."

"The suits (Wands, Pentacles, Swords, and Cups) correspond to their own unique areas of life and astrological elements. Wands symbolize passion and inspiration, Pentacles represent money and physical realities, Swords depict intellectual intrigues, and Cups illustrate emotional matters."

There are a variety of spreads we can use. One card, three card, five card. One card is often good for a yes or no answer while a more complex five card spread can be much more informative. We will use the five card spread today. One other thing. The direction the card is facing in the spread makes a difference. Upright or reversed. Upright is usually a good omen or neutral. Reversed is often bad news. Shall we proceed?"

"Let's get on with it. Wait, I want to shuffle and cut the cards. In fact, I want a new deck!"

"Certainly! Madame Catt, will you do the honors?"

"Of course!" Chita walked over to the small stand and took up an unopened box and brought it over to the table. She handed it to Gaston who tore the seals open, took out the cards and carefully counted and examined them.

"OK, I'm going to shuffle and cut, cut and shuffle. That's something I'm good at." He took the deck in his paws and demonstrated his obvious poker skills. He handed the deck back to the Bichon who proceeded to deal a spread of five cards.

She smiled. "This is something I'm good at or rather, the spirits are good at. I feel their strong presence. Do you?"

A soft rustling whisper issued from the hidden transceiver, barely audible. Ursula was on duty.

Gaston looked around and shook his head. "I don't feel anything. Let's get going here."

Giselle took the deck he had shuffled and cut and dealt five cards from the top. *(carefully and stealthily selected)* The first card was upright and in the Minor Arcana – Pentacles - money and finances! The next from the Major Arcana was a reversed Chariot. That was followed by two more Major Arcana cards both reversed – The Star, the Moon and then the fateful Tower upright.

The Bichon paused, stared at Gaston and said, "I'm afraid the spirits are using the Tarot to tell you of serious problems. The Pentacles mean money. Three of the Major Arcana are reversed. This does not bode well. The reversed Chariot speaks to a loss of control. The reversed Star suggests faithlessness, probably among your staff or customers. The Moon reversed usually implies confusion or fear. Whether that's you or your minions isn't clear. But finally, the upright Tower is the worst case scenario and speaks of disaster. You have a powerful competitor. There may be unwelcome surprises in store that can create a sudden loss of command and resources."

The rustling sound increased in volume and was joined by a gentle moan.

"The spirits are unhappy for you as am I."

Gaston's face was like thunder. Losing his cool, he barked and blurted, "Disaster! Me, Gaston? No way! That's a bunch of superstitious hooey! I'm not some gullible jerk. I don't believe any of this. I am having a few setbacks but that's all. I'm getting to the bottom of it. I've lost a few shipments. My so-called competitor will soon be dead meat. The FBI has nothing on me. My crew is loyal to me. They know better than to screw around. Your spirits are a bunch of phonies. And you're an even bigger phony. Luciano! Come on! We're leaving. Pay these witches. I don't want them hurling any curses my way."

He pushed back his chair, reached out and scattered the Tarot Deck on the floor. "Somebody's paying you to scare me off, aren't they. It's not going to work. I'm going to your new rival and getting the truth."

He stormed out leaving the Mastiff to pay and pick up their weapons.

Luciano winked at Giselle and Chita and followed his raging boss.

When the door to the apartment slammed closed, Otto appeared and the three conspirators plus Ursula gave each other a thumbs-up, shut off the whispering transceiver and set about picking up the cards strewn all over the floor. Ursula had recorded the session and was transmitting it to Special Agent Badger.

Otto checked the door to make sure the dogs had truly gone and then turned to Mlle Woof. "Brilliant, Giselle, just brilliant. In spite of all his bravado, he's really worried and suspicious of his associates. Now we need Round Two with the Wolves to push him over the edge. I'm heading over to the hotel. I'll brief them on how this session played out. I don't know how long it will be before he turns up on their doorstep but I suspect he'll want to get a more favorable reading ASAP. You guys can get ready to vamoose."

He 'zapped' over to the French Quarter Hotel and caught the Wolves just as they were preparing to go out to dinner. "Hey, Otto, we found a place nearby that makes the greatest Jambalaya, Gumbo and Étouffée. We weren't going to travel to New Orleans and not take advantage of the fabulous food. C'mon and join us. Did our Great Pyrenees buddy get the treatment from Madame Giselle?"

"He did indeed and Mlle Woof was sensational. Chita and Ursula set the atmosphere and I spooked them by telekinetically lifting their artillery when they entered. She laid it on him - heavy doom and gloom. He protested. Called her a phony and stomped out but he was rattled. He said he was coming here to get an honest reading. He doesn't admit it but he was shook. The idea that he's working with a bunch of traitors isn't sitting very well. Expect to hear from Luciano shortly. You may have a message already."

Frau Schuylkill said, "Great. The sooner the better. I want to get back to Cincinnati. Have the cosmic travelers left on their next adventures yet?"

"Not yet. I think they're leaving tomorrow. First to Rhea and then to Gaea. The Twins want to meet an H.Sap."

Ilse laughed, "So would I. Wyatt here has had that pleasure but I haven't."

The Colonel smiled, "Speaking of pleasure, here we are. I don't know about you two but I'm up for a big bowl of Gumbo. After dinner, come on back to the hotel with us, Otto. We'll go through our routine one more time. I assume you'll be with us when Gaston shows up."

"Oh, yeah. Wouldn't miss it. I wonder how comfortable a sheep dog will be with a couple of oversized wolves."

Chapter Thirteen

Preparations are finally complete.
And the Twins are just thrilled to repeat
One more trip into space.
They both cover their face
And they hope that they land on their feet.

The Bear's Lair

Octavius here: "Our close neighbor Alpha Centauri is a star 25 trillion miles or over 4.3 light-years from Earth's Sun. It appears as a single point of bright light in our southern sky. It is actually a pair of twin stars (A and B) tightly orbiting each other. A third star, Proxima Centauri, is slightly closer to Earth and is much smaller and dimmer.

A planet orbits one of the twins, Alpha Centauri B, every 3.24 Earth days. It is possibly just a bit bigger than our world, orbiting in a "habitable" zone. We have determined that the planet is Rhea, our next tour objective. Before Otto made the journey, *(See Book 12- The Nut Case)* Ursula had traversed the distance through a wormhole and examined the nature of the planet. Her report follows:

"Envision an exoplanet, smaller than Earth but orbiting at extremely high speeds around its star Alpha Centauri B. It has two moons and the star Alpha Centauri A is clearly visible as well. It has large bodies of water and volcanic islands with little in the way of habitable space. Nevertheless, there is a remarkably close resemblance to our Earth, not just physically, but in the nature of its civilization. For Rhea is populated by a relatively small number of species closely akin to our own. Their overall numbers are miniscule. Homo Sapiens does not exist there. It is not clear they ever did."

"I have been able to identify equines, ursines, felines and other mammalian species similar to those on Earth. There are no reptiles, fish, insects or birds. The inhabitants are mentally capable and self-aware. Most of them speak and write a single language not unlike English with a few dialects. Technologically, they are somewhat behind Earth although some seem to understand space and extra-planetary travel. Several groups are convinced other worlds exist in far-away systems and galaxies. Most Rheans think that is a myth."

The Multiverse Lab at the Bear's Lair was taking on all the hustle and bustle of a busy airline terminal as the travelers got their stuff together and prepared for their jump to Rhea. Octavius, Belinda, Howard and the Twins were putting last minute touches on their baggage. Belinda was giving final instructions to Huntley who really didn't need them. *(He was working out beautifully.)* The Flying Tigers were standing by. They would be joining the team on Rhea as soon as they returned from picking up the card sharps in New Orleans. Otto was still in the Big Easy but would ultimately end up with the tour group either in Rhea or Gaea after making a short detour to Orb to check on the conflict between the Emperor and the Priests. Busy, Busy!!

Two Ursulas were going along as well. A model 13 and a prototype model 14 on a shakedown run. There would be further testing of the model 14's Augmented Reality functions along with the associated headsets and contact lenses courtesy of Byzz Bonobo. The first trial is set for New Orleans.

The Twins were revved up about that prospect. Visions of integrating augmented and virtual reality into their internet games were already bouncing around in their techie heads. They were still of two minds about leaving the games in the care of the Hex geeks. On the one paw, the Twins were delighted with the progress the gamesters were making in enhancing and marketing The Bold Brave Brilliant Bumptious Bears while they were flitting from planet to planet. But they missed the fun of developing new ideas, plots and avatars to upgrade their enterprise. Frustrating but they did want to meet an H.Sap. Oh well!

Arabella squeaked. "I hope we don't land face down again!"

Howard and Marlin were doing some last minute adjustments to the Multiverse systems. Finally, he called the group together. "Are we all set? Any last minute potty calls? Baggage in hand? Priscilla has been alerted to our arrival and is waiting for us. OK, Marlin, let's go!" Whoosh!

The cosmos went black!

Chapter Fourteen

They're in Rhea and all in one piece.
Thanks to Howard's complete expertise.
Ms. Priscilla is there
With her spiny dark hair.
She's the chief politician's young niece.

(Exoplanet Rhea – Prime City)

Thump, thump, thump, thump and thump! Five fur covered bodies landed none too gracefully in the lobby of the Rhean Science Center. They had been holding paws when they began their journey and managed to stay together and upright. This was a major feat since quantum traveling was not a precise process and it was not uncommon for voyagers to miss their targets by a significant distance, land on their heads or both.

Howard was on his feet first. "Is everyone OK?"

Octavius emitted a groan and Belinda was shaking her head. The Twins jumped up and ran toward an attractive Porcupine who was watching the proceedings, giggling softly to herself. "Hi! You must be Lady Priscilla. We're the Octavian Twins - Arabella and McTavish. That huge Kodiak is our Dad and the gorgeous Polar is our Mother, Bearoness Belinda. You know Howard, don't you?"

"Greetings, both of you! I met your parents on Earth and I'm also familiar with Howard Watt. Welcome, one and all! My Uncle Portnoy, Rhea's Chief Executive, is engaged in governmental affairs but he wants me to extend his good wishes and hospitality. He will meet with us later."

Belinda had recovered her savoir faire and extended her paw in greeting to the beautiful Hystricide. "We meet again, Lady Priscilla. This time on your territory. Sorry, I'm still a bit woozy. This is only my second Multiverse journey. Takes a little getting used to."

"I remember my first jump trip to Earth in the not very gentle custody of Otto the Magnificent. Not very enjoyable. Where is he, by the way? I expected he'd be with you."

"He's engaged in an important project on Earth but he'll be along."

We'll also have two more animals joining us shortly. Ben and Gal Tigris. White Bengals who fly my aircraft. The Flying Tigers."

Octavius staggered to his feet and then rose to his imposing nine foot height. *(He had suffered an attack of narcolepsy on the trip and was just waking up.)* "Ms. Priscilla, good day. Thank you and your uncle for your hospitality. We are looking forward to our stay here in Rhea."

"We are delighted to have you. We haven't forgotten your help in ridding our world of the despot Admiral Tumult. This is a new, vital Rhea."

Howard returned after checking on their traveling goods and chattels. "All present and accounted for. Hello, Priscilla! *(slight blush)* So nice to see you again. Thanks for the invitation. How is your uncle?"

"Fine, Howard *(return blush)* Welcome! Uncle is fine and sends his regards. He'll join us later."

The Twins broke in. McTavish looked around. "This place looks really interesting. We love science. Can we have a tour?"

"Of course but let's get you settled and fed first. *(Arabella gave that thought a high-five.)* Then I'll introduce you to some of our staff members. They're interested in meeting animals from Earth and will be happy to give you the full treatment. They'll probably wear you out."

Belinda laughed, "Don't count on it. There's a lot of energy packed in those furball bodies to say nothing of their inquisitiveness. Don't let them get started on their Internet games."

"We have booked you into the Grand Hotel. It's just a short walk from here. It's the only place that has a bed large enough for you, Octavius."

Howard sorted out their baggage and joined Priscilla, Porcupine to Porcupine, as they formed a small procession out of the Science Center and over to the hotel. "How have you been, Howard?"

"Fine, Priscilla. Very busy.. How about you?"

"Very well! Have you given any further thought to joining me here at the Science Center? The job is still open."

Howard

Priscilla

"Sorry, Priscilla. The prospect is tempting but I'm immersed in Octavian projects. Multiverse travel isn't the only thing I manage. Right now, I'm involved in a couple of crime situations and a few other experiments. But maybe while I'm here, we can get together by ourselves. How about dinner tomorrow night."

"I guess it will have to do. Maybe I can talk you into changing your mind."

Howard laughed, "Fine, but I think you ought to start recruiting for a Chief Science Officer from your local associates."

He couldn't completely expunge from his memory the fact that Priscilla had been the tyrannical Admiral's Executive Officer. She had dramatically changed her loyalties when threatened with death by the Zebra. Was she still the hyper-ambitious schemer or had she truly turned the page. He didn't know and while he found her very attractive personally, he didn't entirely trust her. Certainly, not enough to leave the Octavians and move to Rhea and work for her. *(And who knows what else.)*

They reached the hotel and she led the cosmic tourists to the front desk. The manager, a Rhean Raccoon, came out of his office to greet them.

Priscilla smiled at him and said, "Roger, this is the party from Earth that I told you about. Doctor Octavius Bear, his spouse Bearoness Belinda Béarnaise Bruin Bear *(nee Black)* and their twin offspring, Arabella and McTavish. This distinguished porcupine is Doctor Howard Watt. They and an Otter associate who will be joining us later were instrumental in overthrowing Admiral Tumult and his mad schemes. Please give them the full treatment appropriate to such a distinguished group. They are here to tour our planet and learn about Rhean culture and civilization."

The Rhean beamed. "Welcome to the Prime City Grand Hotel. Travelers from Earth! How wonderful! We have reserved our VIP suites for your stay with us. Lady Priscilla, I believe you and your party will be dining with us this evening along with the Chief Executive."

"That's correct, Roger. Later in the week, they will be joined by two Bengal Tigers and the Otter I mentioned. I assume you have provided suitable rooms for them as well."

"It has been seen to, Lady Priscilla. Ladies and Gentlebeasts, if you will follow our commissionaire, he will show you to your suite. Please do not hesitate to call upon me for any of your needs and requests. The Prime City Grand is totally at your service."

Octavius raised himself up to his full nine foot height, towering over the Procyon and said, "Thank you, Mr. Raccoon. I'm sure we will be quite comfortable here. We will probably only call on you to praise your establishment."

They strode off after the bell dog to the VIP elevator.

The Twins, as usual, were overloaded with enthusiasm. Bouncing on the luxurious bed in their room, they shouted into the central living area. "Hey Mom and Dad, when do we get to tour the Science Center? Priscilla is really something."

Arabella squeaked, "I think there's something going on between her and Howard."

McTavish razzed her. "Romance! That's all you females think about. Phooey!"

Arabella pinched his front leg. "Oh, put a sock in it. Whatever a sock is."

Octavius stuck his head into the room. "You'll have plenty of time for touring tomorrow morning. Priscilla and Howard have laid on a full day's worth of activities starting at the Science Center. Right now, get changed for dinner. We'll be eating with the Chief Executive, Priscilla's uncle Portnoy."

Belinda asked, "Does Portnoy have a first name?"

"That is his first name. Sir Portnoy Porcupine. Rheans tend to use first names only unless you are a despotic nut like the Zebra, Admiral Tumult. His first name was Titus. He persisted in being addressed as Admiral. Never commanded a navy, fleet, flotilla, ship or even a rowboat."

"Where is he now?"

"Dead. His body was found floating near an island penal colony that he'd been sent to after he killed his executive officer. We suspect his guards did him in. He was universally hated."

"Well, it sounds like the situation here has vastly improved."

"Maybe but Rhea is still short of living space. A serious problem."

"What do they propose to do about it?"

"That's one of the things I want to find out while we're here. I have good reason to believe that the late Admiral's schemes of planetary conquest were designed, aided and abetted by the Lady Priscilla. He's gone but she's not. Is this Science and Technology Center truly benevolent? Has the Admiral's Company actually been disbanded? How do they plan to colonize supposedly uninhabited but habitable exoplanets. Are their targets truly uninhabited? They have limited Multiverse travel capability but I think it's enough to transport a group of volunteers on a voyage of forcible colonizing.

"Sorry, I may just be paranoid but I wonder how benign their plans and intentions might be toward a partially developed exoplanet like Biosphere K. They could probably overrun the inhabitants and take over whatever infrastructure there is. No doubt all in the name of bringing a higher level of civilization to the world. Dictators have used that wheeze to justify aggression for centuries. Upgrade the noble savages and in the process take over their world and solve our living space problems."

"You make it sound pretty threatening. Any proof?"

"That's what Howard and I plan to uncover. I hope our suspicions are unfounded. I'll be glad when Otto gets here. He and Ursula are marvels at digging below the surface. I also want to probe this Chief Executive Portnoy. Is he the beneficent leader he makes himself out to be?"

Belinda shrugged, "I knew this wasn't going to be just another vacation jaunt. Problems just seem to follow you around. Let's not spoil it for the Twins, though."

Chapter Fifteen

It is time for the Colonel and Frau
To meet Gaston and then tell him how
His world's going to shake.
His whole empire will break.
He's got to control it somehow.

Back in New Orleans, the Wolves plus Otto and the Ursulas were getting ready for Gaston Le Chien. The hotel suite was a model of stark functionality. Bland pictures on equally bland walls. A covered table under a dimmable chandelier. A small stand with several unopened decks of standard cards. A chair poised on each side of the table and several more chairs at the wall where Wyatt and Luciano would sit and observe the proceedings..

The Flying Tigers had made the trip back down to MSY to stand by, ready to take the team back to Cincinnati. At the moment, they were with Giselle and Chita. They had already delivered Ursula 14's Augmented Reality gear to the Wolves – contact lenses especially developed by the Hex technicians. The Artificial General Intelligence system would use them to supply Frau Ilse with interpretive information about the cards that she would pull from the standard 52 card pack. Ursula 14 was housed in the resident hotel TV set. Ursula 13 was up in the chandelier doing backup duty. In addition to supplying spiritual sound effects she would record the session. Otto had taken up a comfortable seat out of sight in an armoire. He was ready to telekinetically disarm Gaston and Luciano once again or confront them, if necessary. The Wolves probably didn't need much help, however.

The room buzzer sounded and Wyatt went to the door. Big as he was, Gaston was taken aback by the sizeable Red Wolf standing in the doorway staring at him with his amber eyes. The Colonel growled. "Mr. Le Chien and Mr. Luciano, I presume. Welcome, Gentlebeasts. Madame Ilse is awaiting you. I must ask that you remove any weapons you may be carrying and leave them here in the foyer before you enter. His formidable gaze allowed of no protest. The two dogs placed their pistols on a sideboard and followed Wyatt. There was a clanging sound as another sidearm fell to the floor next to Gaston. *(Otto was at his telekinetic best again.)*

The Colonel frowned and bared his teeth. "Perhaps I didn't make myself clear Gentlebeasts. When I said, 'any weapons,' I meant 'all weapons.' Please put that revolver with the other guns. Thank you."

Once again, Gaston was clearly alarmed both by the mystical disarmament and the fearsome Canis Lupus. He was even more unnerved when he was presented to Madame Ilse, a Grey Wolf of exceptional size for a female. He looked at Luciano who somewhat theatrically shared his boss' concern. The Mastiff took a seat next to the Colonel.

The Frau smiled, showing her ample mouthful of shining teeth, licked her chops and said in Français de Suisse, *("M'sieur Gaston, M'sieur Luciano! Bonjour! I am delighted that you have seen fit to consult the life-forces through my humble efforts. As I think you know, unlike some other so called cartomancers, I prefer to use the standard deck of playing cards to elicit the spirits' pronouncements. I am sure you are familiar with the 52 cards plus jokers that we use. You may not be familiar with their predictive characteristics. As we proceed, I will call upon the denizens of the afterlife to give us enlightenment.")*

"Let's speak English. Madame. My associate does not understand French. He's Neapolitan. In spite of that, I keep him on. *(chuckle)*"

"Of course. *(Another intimidating smile)* Well, shall we?"

"First of all, I want a new deck and I want to inspect it."

"Certainly! Colonel, would you do the honors?"

"Colonel?? A colonel of what!"

"Don't be concerned, Mr. Gaston. I retired from the Army many years ago. Madame insists on using the honorific. I am Mr. Wyatt Where and have been for quite some time. No affiliations or special relations."

He rose and walked over to the stand and came back with an unopened deck of playing cards. "Yours to open and inspect, sir."

The Pyrenees tore off the cover and took out the contents. He flipped through them looking for marks, shavings, bends and color discrepancies. He shuffled and cut them several times and examined them once more looking for size and thickness differences. He found nothing and placed the deck in front of Madame Ilse.

She laughed. "I see that you are most cautious, M'sieur Gaston. Could it be that you have been cheated in card games?"

"Yes, but the cheater didn't get a chance to collect his winnings. I did learn a lesson from him but he learned an even tougher lesson from me. By the way, just so you know, I went to a rival of yours yesterday for a reading. A Bichon Frisé. Forgot her name. She used Tarot Cards. Damned complicated. I didn't care for her predictions or the cards."

Ilse frowned. "You must mean Madame Giselle. I hear she has taken up residence in New Orleans. I am only here for a few days. I'm on a country-wide tour. She is an utter fraud. Leads her clients on with a supernatural gloom and doom story and then tries to get them back for another reading. We'll use the tried and true playing cards and what the spirits tell us, I will pass on to you fully and unaltered. There will be no second readings. The truth is unalterable. Now I give you a choice. How many cards shall I use? One is good for a 'yes-no.' Three are more revealing and five gives a full picture."

"Five!"

"Excellent! Now what do wish the spirits to divulge for you?"

"I run a large and profitable business that you don't need to know any more about. I've had a few setbacks recently. I want to know why and who's responsible. Once I know that, I'll take the necessary steps."

"That sounds ominous but you are wise to seek guidance. Let us see what the cards will tell us. Please cut and shuffle several times and then pass the deck to me."

While the dog manipulated the cards, Ilse surreptitiously adjusted her contact lenses and Ursula 14 flashed a "Good to Go" image on the Augmented Reality surfaces. He finished and placed the deck in front of her face down.

"Please cut one more time!"

He did a one-paw cut. She smiled. "I see you are an experienced dealer."

Sitting in the corner, Luciano grinned. He wondered if the drug lord would catch the double meaning. Probably not. Subtlety was wasted on the boss.

She reached and took the first card and turned it over. The King of Spades. Ursula 14 flashed a message to the Wolf.

Ilse spoke, "King of Spades indicates a man of bad faith. He is a predator who seeks to use you for his own ends."

Gaston barked. "It's that damned Mexican Ocelot. He wants to take over my business. What's next?"

She took another card, flipped it and announced, "The 7 of Diamonds."

Ursula messaged. "Good. This one is vague. Challenges at work."

The Frau repeated what she saw on her lenses."

Gaston was impatient. "Yeah. Yeah, I know. That's why I'm here."

The next card was the 3 of Diamonds. "Legal problems."

"Those rotten Feds are trying to shut me down. I'd like to see them try. I've got some of the best lawyers in New Orleans."

The fourth card was the 4 of Clubs. Ursula signaled: Deceit or betrayal, potentially by a friend. Ilse passed it on.

"Luciano, you bastard. Are you setting me up?"

The Mastiff woofed. "Don't be ridiculous, Boss. Haven't I been with you through thick and thin? You're letting these stupid readings bend you out of shape."

"Maybe but then who?"

"I don't know. Maybe nobody!"

"We'll see. OK, She-wolf, what's the fifth card?"

"The 10 of Spades! *(intake of breath)* Bad news, worry, imprisonment."

"No way! You're worse than that Tarot dame. Pick one more."

"We've used up our five cards but all right. I'll pick one last one."

"Ace of Spades. Catastrophe!"

Gaston jumped up, threw over the table and stomped out of the room.

*****

Sitting in the back of his Catillac limo, Gaston was in a rage. "Nobody betrays Gaston and gets away with, Luchi. I want the traitors identified today. I'll deal with them after I get rid of that stinking Mexican Ocelot. You think those card readings were a waste of time. They confirmed what I've believed for a long while. I have a rotten competitor who's reached my team. How did the Feds know about our shipments? Did he offer my boys bribes? A couple of them are jealous. They want to be the top dog of an operation. Well, they're going to be dead dogs."

"Maybe they were threatened, Boss."

"They know how to handle threats. So do I. I'm going to personally snuff that Mickey Mouse Mexican. Where does he live?"

"I'm not sure. I'm told he moves around. I think the Algiers district."

"He won't move much when I get finished with him. Find him, NOW!"

He shouted at the chauffeur. "Let's go, Izzy. Luchi! You've got your orders. Don't fail me. You know how I feel about failure and losers."

The Mastiff nodded his head. He knew from experience. He had a few phone calls to make, especially to a tough FBI Special Agent.

Chapter Sixteen

Back in Rhea, a dinner is set
How luxurious these things can get!
The Lord Portnoy holds sway.
He's got plenty to say.
But he's not being truthful just yet.

Dinner at the Moon Vista Restaurant at the Prime City Grand Hotel. Octavius, Belinda, Howard and the Twins were seated with Priscilla and Chief Executive Portnoy. They had gone through aperitifs and were about to attack the appetizers accompanied by the first of several vintage Rhean wines. The Twins were snarfing up delicious fruit concoctions.

"We're most grateful to you, Lord Portnoy for permitting and facilitating our visit here."

"The gratitude is ours, Bearoness. Without the help of your associates, we would still be under the hooves of the tyrannical Zebra Admiral Tumult and his thugs – whom, incidentally we have rounded up and arrested. As you know, the Admiral is dead under mysterious circumstances which I blush to admit we did not investigate very thoroughly. My niece has seen the error of her ways and is making great progress in developing our Science and Technology Center."

Arabella looked over at Priscilla and asked, "Does your planet have a star like our sun?"

"Three in fact, two are bright and close in. One is further out and somewhat dimmer. They're actually a related system. We called them the Triplets. You call them Alpha Centauri. There are other stars in our galaxy but the Triplets dominate. I don't know how you measure time on Earth but Rhea orbits its star far more quickly than it takes you to go around your sun."

Octavius stuck his snout in. "Bella, like Earth, Rhea has seasons with changing weather and growth characteristics. As you know, Earth has four of about even duration: cold Winters; hot Summers; mild intermediate transitional periods- Spring and Fall."

Portnoy chuckled. "I wish ours was that simple. We have eight."

McTavish laughed. "Do you have Christmas twice a year?"

"What's Christmas?"

"Can we tour the Science Center, Lady Priscilla? I want to see your suns and two moons up close.

"Certainly. It's our first stop tomorrow morning. It's nowhere near as sophisticated as what you are used to on Earth but it will give you a good picture of Rhean planetary traits and our problems with overcrowding."

Belinda raised her vestigial eyebrows. "Is the problem that serious? Or was the Admiral simply looking for new worlds to conquer?"

Portnoy responded. "A bit of both, Bearoness. We are indeed looking for possible uninhabited exoplanets to colonize but the Admiral had intergalactic conquest on his distorted mind. He was using our living space problem as an excuse to stir up his followers to invade other worlds, occupied or not. That is not our agenda. We have identified most of his supporters and shut them down. A few still persist, unfortunately. Let us change the subject. I understand that you have a pair of Tiger siblings who pilot your aircraft."

"That is true, Lord Portnoy. I am a highly experienced pilot myself and we own several different types of airplanes from high speed jets to huge freighters along with a fleet of helicopters."

"It sounds like you have more flying machines than our entire planet."

She laughed, "Oddly, our team of Flying Tigers have flown extensively on Earth but this will be their first journey to another world. They have one major trip to make and then they will be joining us."

Priscilla looked at Howard quizzically. "Will Otto be arriving soon? He was the one who helped overthrow The Admiral and The Company."

"I'm not sure. He was quite eager to come back to Rhea but he has a couple of stops to make before he arrives."

Chapter Seventeen

As the seers both prepare to depart,
Having practiced their soothsaying art,
Gaston's all in a rage
He decides to engage
In a shootout. That's not very smart!

The DHC-6-300 Twin Otter stood in the General Aviation area at MSY Airport awaiting its complement of passengers for the trip back to Cincinnati and the Bear's Lair. The Flying Tigers had seen to the refueling and were going through their external and internal checklists when a large SUV drove up to the flight line and unloaded Giselle, Chita, Wyatt, Ilse and Otto. *(along with the omnipresent Ursulas.)*

Otto patted the fuselage of his namesake aircraft as they placed their luggage in the stowage compartment. "Good old girl. Ready whenever we are. I'm glad I don't have to 'zap' back to Ohio. Takes a lot of energy and adrenaline. It's bad enough I have to make three quantum jumps in the next few days. Ursulas, what do we know about the outcome of our card handling capers?"

"Nothing definite yet. We have an open channel to Special Agent Badger, Luciano and Miguel. As soon as Gaston makes a move, the Feds will grab him, preferably on an attempted murder charge. Miguel and Luciano are both wearing bullet proof protection. We'll keep you posted."

The contingent was comfortably seated as the Tigers spun up the engines, contacted traffic control and headed for the active runway. The Frau and Colonel were often in the cockpit but this time they were just relaxing after their exercises in card based divination.

Mlle Woof and Chita were chatting earnestly. Chita's show-biz sense was working overtime. "I see this as a new career for you, Giselle. No more Mlle Governess. We'll tackle Maury as soon as we get back. 'Polar Paradise presents Madame Giselle, Queen of the Tarot.' With Ursula 14 backing you up with augmented reality signals, you will be a sensation with the Shetland tourists. Otto can provide comic relief. "

"I don't want to cheat, hurt or mislead anyone."

"Certainly not. No money involved. No life influencing judgements, predictions or suggestions. I admit I have a history of larceny but I'm proposing entertainment for entertainment's sake. They'll ask, "How did she know that?" We can combine Otto in your act and he can provide some telekinetic effects to wow the audience. Fun, fun, fun! I'll talk to Belinda and Octavius. They'll need to sign off but if Maury buys the idea, I think we'll have a runaway success on our hands. We can work up a dynamite act."

Giselle admitted she was tired of being Mlle Woof and chasing errant furballs. But she felt she was part of the Octavian family and was looking for a way to maintain her status. She loved the Twins but they were growing up and didn't require her constant attention. She'd still be there for them if they needed her. Maybe Chita had the solution. Reading the cards was fun.

On to the Bear's Lair and then later, the Shetlands and Polar Paradise.

*****

The black Catillac limousine pulled up in front of a nondescript house in the Algiers district of New Orleans. Home of Miguel, the Ocelot "drug dealer" in the employ of the FBI. Gaston yelled at the driver. "Izzy, get ready for a quick getaway."

The impulsive and overwrought Great Pyrenees decided he would settle this problem himself in spite of his gang members urging him not to go. "This is between me and that rotten cat. Nobody diddles Gaston and gets away with it. Stay in the car, Luchi."

Luciano was only too happy to comply. Hot head Gaston was about get his comeuppance. He threw his big body against the front door, holding an AK 47 in his paws and screamed. "Come out you b….., meet your doom."

He was greeted by a shout. "Gaston, drop the gun! This is the FBI!" He turned and violently fired off a volley from the automatic weapon. A single shot from a government SWAT member took him down. Dead! As predicted by the Ace of Spades – Catastrophe."

Chapter Eighteen

Lots of thoughts about Giselle's career.
The big plan for her act has come clear.
Otto will be her mate
And her prospects look great
As her move to the Shetlands draws near.

Maury here. The Twin Otter settled gracefully on the runway at the Bear's Lair. After a stop-off in Nashville to refuel, the Flying Tigers had flown the utility aircraft on a straight line course to Cincinnati and the mansion's landing area.

The ground crew, Huntley and I were on hand to welcome the travelers as they piled out of the passenger door. Frau Ilse made a beeline for her beloved kitchens to whip up a restorative feast. The Colonel joined her. Chita, Giselle and Otto accompanied me in the lounge with their own liquid restoratives. On the flight up, Chita and Giselle outlined their plans for 'Madame Giselle, Queen of the Tarot' to Otto who was wildly enthusiastic. He was already thinking up comedy routines to accompany the Bichon's card based predictions. He loved magic and Ursula 14's Augmented Reality would provide the finishing touches.

Next stop was me, Maury or in this case, Talent Agent Maury. "I really like the idea. It will give the Polar Paradise tourists something different in the way of entertainment especially if Otto plays his slapstick off the 'serious' and 'mysterious' Madame Giselle. I know you both have a crazy sense of humor and can work out routines that will tickle the customers. This could be the new career we want for you, Giselle. I'll speak to Octavius and Bel next time we're in contact. Brush up your French, Otto. Giselle, get your Tarot skills polished. You'll need a costume or two. I'll talk to Dougal about setting up a stage for you. We need to get you and Ursula 14 synched up with Augmented Reality. Chita, get those brains churning. Ideas, ideas!"

Otto chirped. "Sounds great to me but first I have a few quantum trips and 'zaps' to make. I have to check in at Exoplanet Orb and see how the

Emperor /Priest conflict is going. Then on to Rhea with the Flying Tigers to join Octavius, Belinda, Howard and the Twins. Finally, we're all going to Gaea and meet a Homo Sapiens. Oh, ladies, I just heard from Ursula. Gaston, the drug lord is dead. I guess that settles that."

The Frau had just re-entered the lounge to announce dinner when she heard Otto's statement. "Ach, Otto, Ursula! Fill us in! What happened?"

Ursula 13 replied. "It seems our Mastiff friend made a few phone calls when he found out Gaston was going to do a repeat of the Valentine's Day Massacre. The FBI showed up at Miguel's house to forestall the slaughter. Instead of surrendering, the drug lord set off a firestorm with his automatic rifle. He was shot dead by one of the SWAT team members. Right now, Luciano and Miguel are on their way to safe houses set up by the Feds in other cities far, far away."

"What about the rest of the gang?"

"Some of them have been pulled in and the rest are under close scrutiny. Drug traffic in New Orleans has a big dent in it for the moment. No doubt, it will start up again."

The Bichon growled. "Well, two good things came out of it. A nasty drug pusher is no more and Frau Schuylkill and I learned how to manipulate cards with Ursula 14's Augmented Reality. I hope Doctor Bear and the Bearoness are willing for Chita, Otto and I to develop our act. Although I suppose I could be a useful detective, too."

I replied, "Don't worry Mlle Woof, sorry, Giselle. You're a full-fledged Octavian and we'll keep you good and busy both onstage and off."

"Thank you, Maury. Or should I say, 'Merci, Monsieur Meerkat'?"

"Whatever the spirits tell you to say."

Laughs all around.

The Frau shook her head. "Come on! Dinner is getting cold."

Chapter Nineteen

The priests kidnap the Princess at night.
Otto rescues her without a fight.
The High Priest is hauled back.
His fate's looking quite black.
And the Merow makes Otto a knight.

Maury here. Otto was in the Multiverse Lab with Marlin and me and on a simultaneous hookup through Ursula with Howard, Octavius and Belinda on Rhea. The Otter had just finished telling them about the New Orleans events and went on to describe the proposal for Madame Giselle, Queen of the Tarot. Belinda, showbear that she is, was delighted with the idea.

"The tourists will go crazy for it. We could start it off as a lead-in to the Aquabears and if, as I believe it will, it catches on we'll make it a stand-alone. You can do double duty, Otto. Breaking up the Aquabears and then being Giselle's foil. What do you think, Tavi?"

Octavius, for all of his capabilities, did not have much theatrical sense but he was smart enough to trust Belinda's, Otto's, Chita's and Maury's show biz experience. He also wanted to reward Mlle Woof's years of service chasing after the Twins. Maybe they could also find her a good part in Preston Pavel Polar's next film spectacular. A cute little white dog surrounded by big white polar bears. After all, she was an actress in Paris. He'd leave that to Maury.

"OK, let's go with it. Maury, you have the lead. We have Otto traveling around the cosmos for the next few weeks. Give me a plan when we get back. Tell Giselle that Bel and I are looking forward to it. Get the Polar Paradise staff and the Aquabears read in. Tell Fiona, Lion and Unicorn. Maybe she can make appearances at their pub and in the Polar Paradise lounge. Does Frau Schuylkill want a show career, too?"

"I doubt it. She's relieved that the whole mess is over."

Needless to say, Otto was pleased and excited. Not quite as pleased and excited about his Multiverse trips but willing to go anyway.

*****

"OK, Marlin, let's get the show on the road or more precisely, me out in space. Master Magician Otto is on his way to planet Orb. I contacted Magister Purre and asked permission to show up. He says I'm welcome. Seems the conflict between the Merow and Leonidas has reached some kind of crisis."

The Dolphin squeaked, "Remember, Otto, you're not allowed to interfere with the internal affairs of the worlds you visit."

"I know. I'm going as an observer. But observers are allowed to comment."

"Don't push it. We can't have you starting a war."

"I think the war may have already started. We'll see. Alright! Out and back. Tell the Flying Tigers to get ready for their first Multiverse jaunt. A different kind of flight to the trips they usually make. I'll be back to join them shortly and we'll go flying down to Rhea. But now, on to Orb and Orient. Ready when you are!"

Whoosh! Darkness! Splat! Otto shook his head and stretched his limbs. "Another hard landing. Ursula, We have to work on that."

"Howard and Marlin are aware of that issue, Otto. Several of the techs at the Hex are running with it."

(Once again, Ursula will be doing translation duty although Otto has picked up a bit of the Orb/Orient language.)

"Ah, you have arrived, Master Magician. Welcome. The Merow is eager to see you."

"Hello, Magister Purre. Good to see you again. Just give me a moment to recover from my journey and I will be at your disposal. How are you?"

"I am as well as can be expected during this conflict. The Merow has banished Leonidas and his Priests to Occident where they have taken up with

94

a few tribal chieftains. I am convinced he is plotting the Emperor's overthrow. Needless to say the Empress and Dowager are sorely distressed. Come, let us go to the Palace. The Merow and the ladies are waiting."

Several guards joined them as they walked toward the magnificent structure shining amidst the trees and water fountains. A few startling notes. Several armored vehicles surrounded the Palace and a full platoon of armed guards was deployed around the perimeter.

"Obviously the military is taking this situation seriously."

"As are we all, Magician Otto."

They proceeded through the stunning corridors to the throne room. The sentinel opened the huge doors and loudly called out: "Your Highness, Magister Purre and the Master Magician from Mediana."

"Send them in immediately."

Empress Catrin and the Dowager were seated flanking the throne. Both were weeping. The Emperor Merow wore a thunderous frown. "Welcome. Magister and Magician Otto. Your arrival is most timely…"

"They have her. They have our wonderful Apricot." the Dowager wailed.

Otto looked at the Emperor who held out a tattered piece of paper. "We just received this. Princess Apricot was abducted from her school last night and is being held in Occident by Leonidas and the tribesmen."

The letter was scrawled in Orb language. Otto surreptitiously passed it in front of his laptop containing Ursula 14. He was wearing the Augmented Reality contact lenses and she sent him a translated copy that appeared in his view:

"Your daughter is our captive. If you wish to see her alive and whole, you will immediately abdicate, swear allegiance to the gods and announce a new theocracy to be headed up by the High Priest Leonidas and his followers. You have twenty four hours. Any attempt to pursue or attack us will result in her immediate and painful death."

"Well," said Otto, "we'll see about that. Your Highness, do you have any idea where they may be keeping her?"

"No, but we do know where Leonidas is hiding out. With one of the more obstreperous tribal sheiks in Occident. I am reluctant to send the army because of their threat to kill our daughter."

"I agree. But acting on my own, I believe I can get her back and possibly deal with Leonidas and the sheik at the same time."

Ursula 14 rang her chime. An Augmented Reality message appeared on his lenses. "Remember the non-interference mandate. We cannot intrude."

"We can handle that after I rescue Apricot. I'm sure that's what Octavius would do. Your Highness, ladies, I am willing to apply my skills in your daughter's behalf and in behalf of your realm. Leonidas is a dangerous fanatic as are his followers. Once I have rescued Apricot, you may deal with them as you see fit."

The Emperor looked at him. "What do you have in mind?"

Otto looked at one of the throne room guards, nodded and whisked him away to the other side of the area. Several of the guards aimed their weapons at him. "Hold tight. Just a demonstration. I plan to find your daughter and teleport her to safety and the back into your loving arms."

The Empress and Dowager were dumbstruck. The Dowager cried out, I saw you do that with a wine bottle. You can do it with people?"

"Yes, your Highness and more than one. Now, where is this mad priest hiding out?"

Magister Purre came forward and showed Otto where across the Great Ocean, the High Priest had his hideout. Leonidas, no doubt, felt secure that the Emperor would be unable to touch him as long as he had Apricot.

The Otter laughed. "A short 'zap' and I can land there. I'll transport Apricot back here and then send Leonidas on a trip back to captivity. What you choose to do with him is up to you. Now, you may wish to send him a return message indicating willingness to negotiate. That will lull him into a sense of triumph and possibly make him careless. I assume he has an intermediary here in Orient."

"One of his priests remains here in the Supreme Temple. He delivered the note. A cheeky churl whose days are numbered."

"Well, send the reply and let me know when he has sent it on to the High Priest. Then I'll take off."

*****

Several Earth *(Mediana)* hours later, the Emperor's spies confirmed that the message had been sent back to Leonidas. Otto tested the directions one more time, checked in with Ursula and 'zapped' across the Ocean onto a sand covered area dotted with substantial tents. Camel-like animals rested at random locations and feline denizens wandered here and there intent on their daily routines. The diminutive otter sneaked up unnoticed to the largest tent and peeked inside. A council of some sort was in progress with Leonidas and a sheik of some authority engaged in active discussion, laced with laughter. In a corner, with her paws bound sat a lovely young cat, head drooping in despair.

He 'zapped' over to her side. She looked up in alarm. "Shh, Apricot. I'm Master Magician Otto. I'm here from your father. The Emperor has sent me to rescue you. Do you trust me?

She looked at him, hesitated and then nodded, Yes,

"Good. Now, I'm going to teleport you back to the Palace. Do you know what teleport means?"

She shook her head, No!

"You'll be flying across the Ocean and back to Orient Palace. Don't be afraid. It's perfectly safe. Only take a few seconds. Your mother, father and grandmother are there waiting for you. Here let me untie you. Don't make a sound. I'll cause a distraction and then send you on your way. Are you ready?"

She paused and then smiled. "OK!"

He gestured toward Leonidas and sent him tumbling over the floor of the tent. He then turned to Apricot and sent her off. The puzzled and concerned tribesmen rushed over to the High Priest and helped him up. He looked over and saw that his prisoner had disappeared. He saw Otto and shouted "You!"

"Yeah, me" He grabbed the High Priest by the paw and 'zapped.'

The Otter and the struggling High priest landed in the Throne Room. Apricot was sitting with the Empress and Dowager, tears running down their faces but smiles on their lips. Two guards seized Leonidas and dragged him in front of the Emperor.

"So, High Priest. You insisted I abdicate, did you? Sorry, It's not going to happen but a major problem awaits you. Kidnapping my daughter, threatening her life, planning my overthrow, colluding with Occident chieftains, attempting to set up a new theocratic government are all acts punishable by death. However, I will throw you on the mercy of the Imperial Justice Courts. The police are here to take you away. You are a disgrace."

"Your letter has been sent to all the Orient and Occident media outlets revealing your shameful demands. Your minions are being arrested as we speak and the Supreme Temple has been sealed and cordoned off. A task force has left for Occident in pursuit of the chieftains who aided and abetted your sordid plan. You are finished, you fanatic"

The High Priest screamed. "The gods will destroy you, you heretic idolator. You and that unspeakable Otter. I will be vindicated."

"Your gods will not be able to help you. There will be no vindication for you. Guards, take him away. Don't be gentle."

As the shrieking prisoner was dragged from the Throne Room, the three females ran over to Otto and smothered him in hugs. The Merow rose from his throne and joined them. He spoke to Otto. "You may have noticed I did not publicize your part in this rescue. I'm sure it is how the gods and authorities of Mediana would prefer it. However, you have my total gratitude and the thanks of my family and my realm. Anything I am capable of providing is yours." He raised his staff. "I dub you Sir Otto the Daring of Orient."

"Thank you, your Majesty. No reward is necessary or expected except your friendship. It is a service any right thinking animal would have provided. It's time for me to return home. Farewell, ladies! Ursula, ping Marlin." A chime, a hum and then a whoosh! The Knight disappeared.

Chapter Twenty

Yes, Sir Otto the Daring is back
But he hasn't had time to unpack.
One more call to assist.
Rhea's next on his list.
He goes off with another wisecrack.

"Welcome back, Sir Otto. Ursula told us the whole story." The Colonel slapped the Otter on the back practically toppling him. The Frau, Chita, Giselle, Marlin, Huntley and the Flying Tigers all joined in a round of applause. "Ursula passed the tale on to Octavius, Belinda, Howard and the Twins on Rhea. They're expecting you and the Tigers tomorrow. The Twins want to include your story in their game - The Bold Brave Brilliant Bumptious Bears starring Sir Otto the Daring of Orient."

"Maury, Is Octavius upset that I interfered in Orient's affairs? I couldn't let that one go. The Emperor's daughter was in danger."

I replied, "No. He's very pleased. You have cemented relations with the power structure of Orb and shut down the renegade Priests. I wouldn't want to be in Leonidas' shoes right now. Does he even wear shoes?"

"Sandals!"

"And those traitorous priests and sheiks either. They're in trouble."

Otto shrugged. "Of their own making. I hope this doesn't descend into open warfare."

"It well might have if anything happened to Apricot. Are they going to let her go back to school?"

"I don't know. I think they'll show a little caution for a while. It's a shame she and the Twins didn't meet. I understand they plan to include my little caper in the next edition of their game."

"Oh yeah. You're an exciting super hero, rescuing royal damsels in distress."

"Ouch. Not sure I want that getting around."

The Colonel and I both laughed, "Sorry, you're stuck with it. Rest up! You have another cosmic jaunt on your schedule."

"Ah, yes. Rhea! Lady Priscilla. I wonder about her."

"What do you mean?"

"She was Admiral Tumult's Executive Officer. I think a lot of his plans of conquest were her doing."

"You don't think she could have turned a page?"

"Maybe. She's Lord Portnoy's niece. What do we know about him?"

"Not much. He seems to be a straight arrow. He'll probably keep her on the up and up."

Otto sighed, "But they still have that overcrowding problem and she's involved in the solution. She also has her eye on Howard."

"Ah, yes. A little cosmic romance. Well, my Lutrine friend, you and Ursula may have a bit of spy work to do on Rhea. Get some sleep."

"No rest for the weary even if I am Sir Otto. Charge!"

"Yeah, Right! Good night, Knight!"

*****

Benedict and Galatea Tigris were pacing the floor after devouring one of Frau Schuylkill's extravagant breakfasts. Never travel on an empty stomach. Otto had just arrived and was munching on a healthy piece of kelp as he led them down the elevator to the Multiverse Lab in the basement of the Bear's Lair. Marlin was at the launch controls with Maury and the Colonel standing by. All three were carrying Ursulas-Models 13 and 14.

"We really don't need to use this takeoff unit. You three are all Adepts and can Quantum Travel on your own power but it's less of a drain on your resources if we give you a boost. Position yourselves in front of the beam. Scrunch down a little, Ben. You, too Gal. Let me check the galactic coordinates one more time. Looks good. OK, Off to Rhea. Bon Voyage. Whoosh!"

Chapter Twenty One

The two Tigers and Otto arrive
With a not very graceful crash-dive.
There's a push on their door
And they're greeted once more
By the Twins with a noisy high-five.

The guests in the lobby of the Rhea Prime City Grand Hotel were taken aback at the sudden boisterous emergence out of nowhere of two large white Bengal Tigers and a small, embarrassed Otter.

"Oh, nuts. I thought we had the coordinates for Octavius' Suite. Try to look nonchalant. I think that female rabbit over there fainted. I hope she'll come around. Let's go over to the reception Desk."

The desk clerk stared but was replaced by the manager who smiled and said, "You must be part of Doctor Bear's party. We had been told to expect you but I was not prepared for your unusual arrival technique."

Otto grinned sheepishly. "Sorry about that. A small navigation error. You may want to see to that distressed rabbit."

The manager nodded to the desk clerk who hastened over with smelling salts to tend to the prostrate Leporid.

"My name is Hairy Otter. *(He refrained from using his recently acquired Knighthood)* This feline lady and gentlebeast are Galatea and Benedict Tigris, White Bengal Tigers from Planet Earth. You are correct. We are associates of Doctor Octavius Bear."

"I am Roger Raccoon, manager of this establishment. Welcome, honored guests! Doctor Bear and his party are out for the moment. I believe they are touring but we have suites prepared for you. As soon as Oswald returns from seeing to that frightened rabbit, I will have him take you to your accommodations. Meanwhile, the good doctor asked us to contact him on your arrival. I shall do so now. Ah, Oswald, has the rabbit recovered? Good! Please take our visitors and their luggage to their rooms. I hope you find them comfortable and to your liking. Lady Priscilla and Lord Portnoy have specifically instructed us that you are to have the full privileges of the house."

Galatea chuffed and said, "Thank you Mister Raccoon. I'm sure we will be most content with your hospitality and facilities. We are highly experienced aviators and pilot Doctor Bear's and the Bearoness's aircraft all over Earth. However, this our first journey off-planet. We are looking forward to exploring your wonderful world and meeting its denizens. Please let our employer know we have arrived."

"I shall immediately. Meanwhile please follow Oswald and relax after what must have been a rather hectic trip."

Benedict growled gently, "You don't know the half of it. Our partner here, Mr. Otter. is a veteran cosmic traveler. We have a lot of catching up to do to match his skills and technique. Oswald, lead on!"

The Tigers shared a two bedroom suite and Otto had a single to himself. No sooner had the clerk left his room after pointing out all the amenities and facilities than a pair of fur covered rockets shot through the still open door.

"Uncle Otto! Hi Uncle Otto! Welcome to Rhea. Mom, Dad and Howard are down the hall visiting with the Flying Tigers. Our suite is on the end and Howard's is next to yours. We heard you were very brave and rescued a princess on Orb. We're going to put that adventure in the next version of The Bold Brave Brilliant Bumptious Bears starring Sir Otto the Daring of Orient. Peer of the Realm. That is, if it's OK with you?"

"Yeah, it's fine, kids. How are your tours and explorations going?"

Arabella enthused. "Great! We went to the Science and Technology Center this morning. They have hydroponic farms. A chemistry and biology lab. Some medical research. A telecommunications and computing center. They've got a lot of star maps and astronomy equipment including a couple of big telescopes. They're searching the sky for new stars and exoplanets."

McTavish looked sheepish *(instead of bearish)* and said, "I made a discovery. I haven't told Howard or Mom and Dad yet. Promise not to tell them until I do. I wandered off while Bella was looking in the telescopes and

I discovered a large room filled with familiar instruments and equipment. One of their techies saw me and shooed me out of there. Restricted area! I didn't think much of it until it dawned on me. The place looked exactly like our Multiverse Lab back home only bigger. You could fit twenty or thirty animals on the launch platform and the projector was huge. You know me and technology. I think they're getting ready to stage a big quantum jump somewhere."

Otto scrunched up his nose. "Well, they are talking about colonizing uninhabited exoplanets to relieve their overpopulation but I didn't realize they were that far along in development. It's dinner time. Let's talk it over with your parents and Howard over food. Unless Priscilla is joining us. If she is, let's keep your discovery to ourselves for the moment."

Unfortunately, she did join them. During dinner, she outlined the next few days' programs. A tour of several schools; interviews with journalists and media celebrities and a meeting of female and medical notables with Belinda, Galatea and Arabella. McTavish, Octavius, Benedict, Otto and Howard were scheduled to meet and greet some Rhean sports luminaries.

There were no sessions arranged with the religious hierarchy. Given their recent run-ins with Leonidas on Orb, this came as a bit of relief for the Great Bear and Otto. Then an evening reception with members of the Supreme Council hosted by Chief Executive Portnoy. Typical events for distinguished guests. A special one-on-one meeting was scheduled between Octavius and the Council member for Defense later in the week.

They thanked the Porcupine profusely for all of the attention they were receiving as well as the efforts for their comfort. Arabella asked if they could spend some time visiting the countryside outside of Prime City and Priscilla made a note to include a helicopter flight on their agenda. All told, it was going to be an exhausting but comprehensive week.

Otto had primed Octavius about McTavish's discovery and they agreed to meet back in the VIP Suite that he and Bel were occupying. Howard had the Ursulas do a sweep for surveillance devices and they uncovered several bugs and clandestine cameras. Octavius was outraged but agreed to stay cool. "Ursula, can you generate a virtual reality scene of the empty room for the benefit of these spy devices. Also please see if you can blank out what they're already recorded."

The AGI did her thing and rang her chime. "Behold the empty room and blanked recordings."

"Thank you! Otto, can you surreptitiously follow Priscilla with another Ursula? I'm getting suspicious. I think she and maybe her uncle are pursuing a hidden agenda and we won't like it."

"I think you're right. I suspect they've hit some kind of an obstacle with their quantum jump program and they need Howard to straighten it out. She's tried feminine wiles. No sale! I'm afraid they're going to use more extreme measures. I may be getting paranoid but I believe another kidnapping might be in the offing. Let's see what I can find out. If I'm right, we ought to blow out of here double quick."

Octavius turned to Howard who was listening to all this. "Where do you suppose they got the quantum jump technology? I doubt they have the in-house capabilities."

The porcupine replied, "My money is on General Turmoil. He wouldn't work with the Admiral but Priscilla and Portnoy may have sold him a bill of goods about searching for uninhabited exoplanets. He may have sold them an even bigger bill of goods. Remember how he tricked the birds on Biosphere X - Home World. That sneaky owl, Mattingly." *(Book 15 – A Case for the Birds.)*

"You may be right. Otto, can you and Ursula do your undercover act?"

"Sure thing. A couple of 'zaps' and we'll be on it." He disappeared holding a small smart phone in his paw – home of Ursula 13.

Ursula scanned for Priscilla's phone and located her in Portnoy's office. Otto 'zapped' the two of them into a corner behind a file cabinet. Ursula went into passive record mode. General Bill Bison, the Councilor for Defense was there. He was speaking. "Well, we're dead in the water without that software. You say those transit algorithms are faulty?"

Priscilla replied. "Not just faulty and buggy. There are major routines missing completely and our techs are at a loss. They're in over their heads."

Portnoy whined, "Go back to that damn General Turmoil. We paid a lot for that rig. Get him to fix it."

She squeaked "He insists the software was complete and functioning perfectly when he sent it to us. He says it must be something we did on installation. He refuses to send another download."

"We should never have trusted that equine lowlife."

She held up her paws. "What choices did we have? It was him or Octavius Bear. And we know how the Bear feels about planetary conquest."

The Bison snorted. "Our invasion force is primed to attack Gaea. That smokescreen of colonizing uninhabited planets will only last so long."

Portnoy whined again, "We need an advanced and inhabited world to take over. Starting from scratch on a desolate rock is too expensive and uncertain. We have troops, not colonists."

The Bison agreed. "Gaea is perfect. Their defenses are marginal. They do have good technology. The government is divided. We can take them. But we have to get our forces there. So what do we do?"

Portnoy grunted, "We use forceful persuasion. Our invitation to that pompous bear and his entourage was well timed. If we can't use inducements or seduction on Howard Watt to repair our system, we'll have to resort to more powerful measures. Those Twins are attractive little buggers, aren't they? I'm sure Howard is very attached to them and wouldn't want them to come to any harm. Let's hold them for ransom. I think our porcupine friend will be all too willing to give us a hand."

She squeaked again, "I'm not sure I want to cross Octavius Bear. Once around with him and his associates was enough. He and his wife are formidable and they have those two huge tigers with them. That Otter is a real threat." The General laughed. "I think my team can handle two bears and a couple of tigers. We'll just stomp on the otter. A threat? Ridiculous. Leave it to me." Otto whispered to Ursula. "OK, I've heard enough. Back to the boss." 'Zap!'

Chapter Twenty Two

Leader Portnoy's an unabashed liar
And he raises Octavius' ire.
They had planned cosmic war
But their weapon's no more.
It's consumed in a volcano's fire.

In The VIP Suite with Ursula 14's Virtual Reality blocking vision and sound, Otto had Ursula 13 play back the conversation they captured in Portnoy's office. Octavius was all action.

He growled, "OK. First we get Howard and the Twins out of here and back to the Bear's Lair. No more kidnappings and hostages. Belinda, go with them. Just grab your stuff and go. Take an Ursula with you. Now"

"I am going to pay a visit to Chief Executive Portnoy and confront him and his sleazy companions. I want the Tigers and Otto with me. We'll follow you shortly to the Lair where we can get ready for our jump to Gaea. They need to know about Rhea's invasion plans which hopefully we can thwart permanently. And before anybody reminds me, I know we are interfering in the affairs of other worlds. I don't care."

An infuriated Kodiak is not a pleasant sight. He waved at Galatea and Benedict to follow. He turned to Otto. "Well, come on. You're obviously not a threat to that Bumbling Bison but I thought you and Ursula would want to be in on the clash."

Otto chuckled, "Yeah, how could I possibly be a threat. Little old me! A small river creature. I think I'll head to the Science Center while you're entertaining them in Portnoy's office. Ursula can keep me up to date."

"Fine. Watch your back!"

"Always!"

As soon as Belinda, Howard and the Twins flashed out of the room and back to Earth, the Bear and Tigers stormed out of the hotel to the Prime City offices of the Council.

Roger Raccoon was taken aback and reached for his telephone. "Lady Priscilla, I think you may have a problem with the Earth party. I'm not sure but that gigantic Bear and his twin Tigers just marched out of here looking quite angry. I don't know where the rest of his party is."

"Thank you, Roger. Where are they headed?"

"I'm guessing either to your Center or the Chief Executive's offices."

She disconnected and thought for a moment. She picked up her phone again, dialed and said, "Give me General Bison. Not there? Find him! Tell him to meet me at Councilor Portnoy's offices immediately. It's critical."

One more call. "Uncle? Priscilla! I think Octavius Bear is heading your way along with his two huge Tigers. He seems to be in a real state. I'm coming over and I've alerted the General. I don't know. He may be aware of our plans although I can't imagine how. I'll be there shortly."

She pawsed. Roger didn't mention the Otter. If the Bear is aware of their kidnapping plans, that damn Lutrine is probably responsible. She rushed out of the Center and skittered the short distance to the Council building. She arrived to see the gigantic Kodiak and his two feline confederates brushing past the guards and receptionist and heading for Portnoy's office. She made it to the portal just in time to see one of the Tigers tear it open. They stormed past a frightened secretary and pulled open the interior door. The Porcupine rose from his desk. "What's the meaning of this, Doctor Bear?'

"Shut up and sit down, Portnoy. Oh, I'm glad to see you here, Lady Priscilla. Where's your other conspirator? The General? Well, never mind. Since you saw fit to bug our rooms, I thought I would return the favor. Care to hear what we discovered?"

Ursula rang her chime and the playback began. It's tough to tell with porcupines but the blood ran from their faces as they listened to themselves plotting away. He ended the recording and said, "Gaea has been warned and Howard, my children and the Bearoness are safely back on Earth."

At that moment, General Bison blundered into the room with several armed soldiers. "Hands up, Doctor Bear, you're under arrest."

His jaw dropped as the trio disappeared on their way back to Earth.

108

Priscilla shook her head. "Don't bother. They're gone."

The General dismissed the soldiers and said, "Let's discuss this. So they warn Gaea. So what! We beef up our offense. Lady Priscilla. We need that Quantum Projector fixed pronto."

Priscilla wasn't paying attention, "Where the hell is the Otter?"

Portnoy squeaked, "Priscilla, concentrate. What difference can an Otter make?"

Her phone rang. Her assistant! "What? Just a moment. I'm putting you on the speaker. The Chief Executive and Defense Councilor are here. Repeat what you just said!"

The voice howled, "I can't understand it. A small animal came running through here and then disappeared. The next minute all our telescopes and star maps vanished."

"What about the Quantum Projector?"

"It's gone too. The entire restricted area is empty except for the technicians. Everything is missing."

She laughed woefully and collapsed. "That, gentlebeasts, is the difference an Otter can make."

*****

A tiny grey figure touched down head first in the Multiverse Lab at the Bear's Lair. Thump! "Hey, Marlin, When are you guys going to improve the landing procedures."

"Howard and Belinda laughed. The Twins jumped on him. Octavius and the Tigers each had a drink bowl in their paws. "Welcome back, Sir Otto! How about a celebratory shot of fermented kelp juice. Mission accomplished?"

"Yes sir, as usual. I'm sure that volcano made a meal out of all that hardware."

"Well done! Drink up! Next stop Gaea. The Twins want to meet a Homo Sapiens. So do we all.

Chapter Twenty Three

Our Giselle is the next Tarot Queen
With her startling magic routine.
To the Shetlands she flies
Through high altitude skies
In the SST soaring machine.

The Aquabear Concorde levelled out at 60,000 feet on its high speed run over the Atlantic, first to London Gatwick and then on to Abeardeen Airport in the Shetlands. Frau Ilse Schuylkill and Colonel Wyatt Where were in the cockpit of the SST. They were both highly experienced pilots but with the arrival of the Flying Tigers on the scene, they got fewer and fewer opportunities to take the Aquabear through its supersonic paces. They were enjoying themselves.

First stop on today's trip was to return Chita to her London based enterprises after her stint in New Orleans. Also on board and heading for Polar Paradise, the Bearoness' castle/resort, was Mlle Woof now about to take up full time employment as Madame Giselle, Queen of the Tarot, entertaining the Polar tourists each evening in the Lounge and Show Room.

The Cat and Bichon had squeezed onto the narrow flight deck, each with a bowl of champagne in paw. "Sorry, we can't offer you two a drink but we want to make sure we got there in one piece." With the plane on automatic pilot, Wyatt leaned back and said, "Never fear, Madame Catt. We are quite competent and highly disciplined. So tell us, what did we accomplish in New Orleans besides learning how to read cards."

Giselle barked, "A nasty drug lord is no more and his operations have been smashed. That's pretty good for a few day's work. And speaking of work, I have the opportunity to start a new career as an entertainer. Everyone has been so helpful. Actually, I'm renewing my theatrical history. I was briefly an actress in Paris but bookings were few, earnings were small and when the Bearoness asked me to take on the Twins, I jumped at it. Now, they're growing up and I can return to my first love, acting and performing. Would you like me to read your destiny, Mon Colonel?"

"Not right now. I have this aircraft to attend to but I'm sure you'll be a smash. I understand you and Otto are putting an act together."

"If Otto ever gets back from cosmos hopping. I understand they made a quick return from Rhea just as we were taking off. What was that all about?"

Ilse chuckled. "A spot of trouble. Check with Ursula. She'll fill you in. She was part of the activity. Now, we are approaching London Traffic Control and we'll be a bit busy up here. Please get a refill and take your seats."

Giselle looked over at Chita. "I don't know how to thank you for suggesting and helping me plan this new career. You have a wonderful imagination and such cosmopolitan knowledge."

"It's what I do, my dear. I'll be stopping up at Polar Paradise to help plan your act, rehearse, flatten rough spots and lead the cheering crowd. Don't forget. You're going to have Ursula 14 and her Augmented Reality techniques to help you along. To say nothing of Otto and his tricks. You'll have the yokels mystified and wanting more. Guaranteed."

Ilse announced they were on final approach. They buckled themselves in waiting to land. They would only be making a brief stop at Gatwick before heading to Abeardeen. Touchdown! Droop snoot lowered.

As they rolled up to the waiting airstairs, Chita winked at Giselle. "I'll say, 'Au revoir' for the moment but I'll see you again very soon."

Wyatt opened the fuselage door and she sashayed out holding her bags. "So long, folks!"

The door was resealed. Wyatt returned to the cockpit and the engines roared back into life.

As they taxied off, Giselle felt like she was the luckiest dog alive. On to the Shetlands, Polar Paradise and her new career. Meanwhile, "Ursula, what happened in Rhea?" The AGI chuckled and played back the events of the day. The Bichon was dumbstruck. "Mon Dieu! No matter where they go, there's trouble. I wonder where they are now.

Chapter Twenty Four

On to Gaea and who can foretell?
Will they meet with another bombshell?
Is this trip one big trap?
How about the H. Sap.?
This adventure is bothering Bel.

The Twins were bummed out by their rapid departure from Rhea. Octavius and Bel did not see fit to enlighten them about their near miss with kidnapping. They pretended there was a problem back at the Bear's Lair that needed their immediate attention.

"OK, kids! False alarm. Huntley has everything in hand. Chita and Mlle Woof are off on the Aquabear to the UK with the Frau and Colonel in control. We'll be leaving for Gaea in the morning. Sorry about the shortened stay in Rhea."

"That's alright, Dad. We're looking forward to meeting an H.Sap on Gaea. We weren't crazy about Rhea, anyhow."

Little did they know. Octavius was sure of one thing. He and Howard wouldn't be going back to Rhea any time soon as long as Portnoy, Priscilla and that blowhard general were still active and in charge. Good ole Otto. Scored again. With no Quantum Jump hardware and software, Rhea's invasion plans were in the dumpster for the near future.

He'd have to have a serious session with General Turmoil. Was he aware of what Rhea intended to do with the technology? You never could tell with that erratic Horse. He certainly didn't prove very helpful to the birds of Biosphere X. Octavius wondered where the mysterious Mattingly Owl was hanging out nowadays. *(See Book 15 – A Case for the Birds)* Was he still working for the General? Who knows? Anyway, anyway!

*****

Seated in the Lair's Lounge, Belinda was getting quite uncomfortable with her cosmic travel and with their whole retirement program. Starting with Australia, then Orb and now Rhea, trouble just wouldn't leave them alone. How about a nice relaxing sojourn on a distant planet without any dire developments. Was that asking too much? She thought not but it didn't seem likely. Next stop, Gaea. Hmm! She looked over at Octavius who was stretched out on a long settee.

"Tavi, I'm having serious second thoughts about this whole sabbatical. Everywhere we go, we seem to run into issues. Maybe this wasn't such a great idea. Australia, Orb, Rhea. Incidents, incidents, incidents! I wonder about Gaea. Will that be safe?"

"I can't swear to it, Bel. You must admit it's been interesting, even exciting so far. The Twins are having a ball in spite of the problems. They have their hearts set on meeting H. Saps. It may be their only chance."

"They'll probably want to include them in their game. At this point, they have enough additional new characters and adventures to create a totally new one. Starring Sir Otto the Daring of Orb. I wish their game wasn't so damned successful. OK, tell me more about our trip to Gaea."

"Well, Byzz has been very busy *(no pun)* getting things set up for us. Remember what she said? Ursula, do you have it?"

The AGI rang her chime and the voice of the Bonobo played back: "I've been keeping up my relations with my former co-workers and management at the Center. I'll get the Director, who oddly enough is a bear, to arrange clearances, a welcoming committee and all that jazz. I'll make sure you meet a couple of H. Saps. They're very interesting. You make your journey to Rhea and I'll get everything set up on Gaea and forward the information to you through Ursula."

Belinda said, "So now, we're back here at the Lair. Let's call Byzz and get an update. Can you bring her up on the screen, Ursula?"

"Just a moment, Bearoness. I'll have to pull her away from the Ursula 14 program. That's working out well, by the way."

A pause. A hum and a brief flash on the big screen followed by a smiling simian face. "Hi folks. I didn't realize you were back in town. I thought you were still on Rhea."

Octavius snorted, "No, we had a little incident and left early. It seems the Rheans had plans of hostile conquest and Otto stopped them in their tracks, so to speak."

"That sounds like a story I'd like to hear. How is everybody? Are the Twins still up for meeting H. Saps?"

As if on cue, the furry whirlwinds bounced into the lounge, looked up at the screen and shouted, "Hi Byzz. We're all ready for Gaea. Are you coming?"

"No, I've been there several times but I have things all set for your trip. You'll be met by the Director of the Telecommunication and Computing Center. He's a Grizzly Bear who says he knows you, Octavius. His name is Grigor Gregory." *(See Book 4 – The Lower Case)*

"Aha, so that's what happened to him. I met him in Winnipeg under, let's say, uncertain circumstances. He was and I guess still is, an electronic whiz."

"Oh yes, quite technically brilliant. I enjoyed working for him but I'm much happier working for Senhor Condor here at the Hex."

Belinda frowned, "Is there any hard feelings between this Grigor and you, Tavi?"

"I don't think so, Bel. We parted amicably. I think bygones are bygones or he wouldn't be willing to welcome us. He left Earth rather rapidly with another Gaean. He's a Multiverse Passive and needed assistance. He hasn't been back here since, has he, Byzz?"

"Not that I know of. He seemed quite eager to see you again."

Bel was dubious but remained silent.

McTavish blurted. "So when are we going?"

"Soon. Keep your fur on!"

*****

Maury here. The Multiverse travelers assembled in the Lab – Belinda, Octavius. The Twins, Howard, Otto and the Flying Tigers. After their foreshortened stay at Rhea, the Bengals were eager to have a real stay at a true exoplanet. Once again I declined the privilege of Quantum Jumping. Byzz had contacted Grigor Gregory through Ursula and he had a welcoming committee standing by at the Telecom and Computing Center.

"Once more unto the breach, dear friends!" No, not Shakesbear's Henry the Fifth but the hum and whoosh of the Multiverse Projector aiding the adept travelers on their journey. Wonder of wonders! Eight *soft* landings in the lobby of the Gaean Telecom and Computing Center reception building. Had Marlin and Howard made the fix or was it just dumb luck? Octavius had stayed awake. Belinda arrived with all her jewelry intact. Howard once again counted noses and baggage. Otto did a series of backflips to work out the kinks and the two twosomes – Bengals and Bears – rose from the floor with as much dignity and sprightliness as they could muster.

A tall Grizzly Bear watched them and then moved forward accompanied by a female Gazelle and *(Ta-Da!)* a male Homo Sapiens. Stares by both parties. On one side, a nine foot Kodiak; a gorgeous Polar Sow; two sets of unusual twins, Feline and Ursine; a Porcupine and a capering Otter. On the other, two animals, Bovid and Ursine, and a Man, never before seen live and in the flesh by any of the Earthlings.

The Grizzly reached over and shook paws with Octavius. "Doctor Bear, we meet again. Never thought it would happen. Winnipeg seems like centuries ago. And this lovely lady is no doubt, the Bearoness. Welcome! Welcome to all of you. Gaea is pleased to have you with us. Byzantia Bonobo has worked with us in arranging your stay. We hope you will be pleased."

"But where are my manners? May I present my Personal Assistant, Jill Gazelle and one of our esteemed technical directors, Harvey Wise. Harvey, as you no doubt have surmised, is one of the many Homo Sapiens that populate Gaea. Young ursines, he will be more than willing to answer all of your many questions as soon as you stop gaping."

Laughter, some of it embarrassed, on all sides.

"Jill has agreed to act as your guide and helper during your stay. She is most efficient and anxious to become acquainted with friendly offworlders such as yourselves. Unlike that wretched Cassowary who was sneaking around our planet seeking to destroy Earth and us. I understand Byzz saw to his final disposition."

"We have arranged lodging for you all at the Center's Hotel. As you might imagine, we have a constant flow of visitors to our launch and technology facilities and we have a substantial housing program to accommodate them. You have deluxe rooms waiting for you. Jill and Harvey will accompany you."

"We have laid on a dinner this evening and two members of the National Legislature, the Vice-President and the Secretary of Defense will be joining us. They are eager to meet you. Your reputations have preceded you. You too, young Bear Twins. Your game, The Bold Brave Brilliant Bumptious Bears, is quite popular here on Gaea. Did you know that?"

McTavish and Arabella beamed. The Bold Brave Brilliant Bumptious *Beaming* Bears.

Grigor smiled, "Doctor Bear, perhaps after you are checked in and settled, you will join me in my office for a drink? Jill can direct you. We will see the rest of you at dinner."

They picked up their bags and trotted off after the Gazelle and Man. Belinda was a bit miffed at being left out of the pre-dinner libations. "What's that all about?"

Octavius replied, "I suspect he wants to review the bidding on his post Winnipeg activities. *(See Book 4 – The Lower Case)* Some of it will be confidential. Don't worry. I'll clue you in on whatever I can and Ursula will be with me."

"See that you do. I love mysteries but only when they don't involve you, me or the Twins."

"Ursula will record all and tell all."

"I'll hold the both of you to that."

116

Chapter Twenty Five

Grigor has a long story to tell
He is home and he's doing quite well
But the fierce Wolverine
Who's exceedingly mean?
That's a tale that is bound to repel.

Grigor's office was large and loaded with technology. Screens of all sizes and orientations dotted his desktop. Photos of rocket launches, antennas and mini-satellites filled the walls and of course, the inevitable white board covered with formulas and notations occupied one long wall. A credenza sat next to his desk with several bottles and cut glass tumblers. Several padded oversize swivel chairs were clustered around a circular table. He gestured for the Great Bear to take one of the seats and picking up two glasses from the credenza he asked, "What's your pleasure, Octavius? Gaean Scotch, brandy, rum. Sorry, no mead! Bees don't inhabit our planet."

"No problem Grigor, I brought my own supply. Unfortunately, it's back in my suite. Brandy will be fine."

The Grizzly poured two generous shots, passed one to Octavius and settled into a companion chair at the table. Octavius put down his laptop with Ursula recording in passive mode.

The Great Bear took a healthy swig and stared at Grigor. "What did you want to see me about, in private."

"You know I left Winnipeg in a hurry with Werner *(Real name Woodrow)* Wolverine after the Canadian police closed in on the deaths of Honoria Heifer and Felicia Foxx. I had nothing to do with either murder but I did assist in a cover up for the Opera Director. I thank you once again for your assistance and getting me legal help."

"My pleasure."

"But it was clear that by staying on Earth I would expose the Gaean observation team that we had established. Honoria wanted more recognition and compensation. The cow had an incredible ego but few brains. She

117

threatened to blow the whistle. The Wolverine had and still has a quick temper and after she refused to return to Gaea, he killed her. Felicia figured it out and tried a little blackmail. Farewell Felicia Foxx.'

"The RCUP *(Royal Canadian Unmounted Police)* had picked me up as a prime suspect and Woodrow worked hard to get himself arrested so he could get near me and take me with him when he quantum transited back to Gaea. He's an adept. I unfortunately am a passive and need an adept or equipment to travel the Multiverse. We escaped."

Octavius smiled, "I knew most of that and figured out the rest. I suspect there is more to your story."

"There is! When we got back here there was an investigation of Honoria's death. Felicia was an Earthling and beyond Gaean authority. I was fully exonerated and the authorities dropped Woodrow's case for insufficient evidence. A number of our Earth team were called back and replaced for safety's sake."

"I joined the Telecom and Computing Center and just recently worked my way up to Director."

"Congratulations. What has happened to our Wolverine friend?"

"He hasn't been so lucky. There have been strong suspicions that he actually is a vicious killer and he has been having trouble getting steady work. You remember he was Director of the Winnipeg Opera and quite a social and political wheeler-dealer. Nothing like that here on Gaea. I haven't had much contact with him but when I do, he is always enraged about his fate. He feels it was his civic duty to do away with Honoria but the good and the great who know what he did don't see it that way. He's a pariah."

Octavius snorted, "I guess I'm sorry about that but I never much cared for him."

"Most people, including me, don't. I tried to get him a job here at the Center but he blew the interview. Anyway, long story short. He's gone rogue. I believe he was tied in with the Cassowary who was plotting to cripple Earth's GPS system. Of course, that bird is dead and the betting is that Woodrow has fled to Rhea. We could use your expertise to track him down."

Octavius winced, "Let's discuss it tonight at dinner. Rhea's a threat."

*****

Back in the suite, Belinda, Howard and Otto listened to the conversation being played back by Ursula. Jill and Harvey had taken the Twins and Tigers for a tour of the satellite launch pad.

Howard spoke first. "Well. That pretty much confirms what we thought. What's the Wolverine up to at Rhea? Was he going to take part in the invasion?"

Octavius nodded. "I suspect so. I'm sure he has it in for a number of folks here on Gaea and wants to take out revenge. He's that kind of character."

Belinda frowned. "So, what do we do? Now that our clever friend Otto has destroyed Rhea's quantum jump gear, are they still a menace?

The Great Bear replied, "Not for the moment. I still have to persuade General Turmoil to cut off their replacements. But let's not get complacent. Those Rheans are a determined and competent lot."

Otto grinned, "Not to forget, downright nasty."

Howard cringed at the thought of Priscilla.

Belinda looked up. "Goodness, it's getting close to dinner. The kids and Tigers should be returning shortly. We'll have to dress up if we are meeting the government heavyweights. Jewelry in full array. Are you going to tell them about Rhea?"

Octavius said, 'Oh, yes! I'll leave it up to them as to how they'll deal with it. For one thing, I expect they'll try to get the Wolverine back here. They could probably make a case for treason if he's actually conspiring with Portnoy and his ilk."

The door flashed open and the Twins bounded in followed by Galatea and Ben. An exhausted looking Gazelle and an amused H. Sap took up the rear.

Arabella giggled. "We were all over the satellite launch pad. Not Cape Canaveral but not bad either. *(See Book 7- The Suit Case)* I'm afraid we wore out poor Ms. Gazelle and Mr. Wise."

McTavish shouted his usual query. "When's dinner?"

Belinda growled, "Soon. Get dressed. Good clothes and no mess." She turned to the two Gaeans. "Will you be joining us?"

Jill said, "Yes we will. Harvey and I will have to dress up. We see lots of government officials but seldom the Vice-President. You folks are special."

Harvey grinned. "And quite a variety. Tigers, Otters, Porcupines and amazing Bears! Those Twins of yours are so smart, they're frightening."

Belinda laughed, "They scare us too. Well, we'll see you at dinner. I am so looking forward to meeting the Vice President and the other notables."

"I think you'll enjoy them. They'll certainly enjoy you. So long, kids!"

McTavish waved "So long, Harvey. Thanks to you and Jill for the tour. Oh nuts! We have to dress up."

Arabella thought that was a great idea. Her brother didn't.

Chapter Twenty Six

The Vice President comes on quite strong.
Her companions are tagging along.
An exchange of views,
Some unsettling news
About Rhea and what could go wrong.

Soft music in the background in the Sky Room. Subdued lighting and large window views of the lights of the Tech Center complex. Members of the wait staff were circulating with trays of beverages and nibbles which the Twins set about devouring. Grigor, Jill and Harvey formed a sort of welcoming committee.

The Vice-President, legislators and Defense Secretary arrived with a security contingent. The Octavians had their own informal security with Otto, Howard and the Ursulas. The Flying Tigers, Bel and Octavius all presented a formidable self-protective image. Arabella and McTavish were their bubbly selves.

Grigor started the introductions. The VP was a Female – Marie Leonore - a Lioness of a certain age. With her short white beard, piercing amber eyes, erect ears and massive jaws she was a daunting figure. She presented her paw to Octavius and then the Bearoness, looked carefully at Howard and Otto as if she realized there was more to those two than one might first imagine. Then she nodded to the Flying Tigers, feline to felines, winking at Galatea who winked back. Finally she took in the Twins who were staring at her in awe. She gave a subdued roar. "Welcome to Gaea, young ones. I don't get to see youth very often. Always ancient stuff shirts like these three." She laughed. "Just kidding! She presented the two legislators and the Defense Secretary. A male and female H. Sap and a War Horse looking very military in spite of his civilian attire. She slapped him on the back. "Meet Mr. Jim Wiley, Ms. Laura Fisher and Secretary Edward Equid."

Belinda and Octavius had the same thought. These were persons to be taken very seriously, especially the VP.

The Lioness looked at Grigor and said. "I've been hearing very good things about you and your organization. Did we actually do something right and select the right animal? Amazing! Introduce me to these two beings."

Jill came forward and accepted the extended paw in her two hooves. "Jill Gazelle, Ms. Vice-President, the Director's Personal Assistant and this is Project Director, Harvey Wise in charge of the Satellite Program."

"Delighted. But I think these two juveniles will starve to death if we don't sit down and start dinner."

She put down her glass and sat at her assigned seat. She winked at the Twins. Arabella giggled. McTavish was looking around for their waiter. The Gaean Security team had taken seats at a side table which still gave them ample access to their charges if their help was needed. They started their pre-set dinners, keeping their eyes peeled on the main table and its occupants.

Octavius and the Bearoness flanked the VP. "You two are quite famous. I feel like I should be asking for your autograph, Bearoness and perhaps a signed scientific treatise from you, Doctor Bear."

"I'll be happy to send you one, Madam. We do have something we want discuss with your party after we eat."

"Oh No! You're not going to try to sell us some UUI technology."

"Hardly. We want to give you some vital national security information."

"Sounds ominous. But let's not ruin our digestion just yet. Where's the waiter?"

*****

The dishes and cutlery were cleared and the waitstaff had withdrawn leaving the diners still seated at the table with their wine glasses topped off. The security team stayed alert at their positions. The twins decided they had better things to do than listen to governmental conversations and asked to be excused. Belinda kissed them both and sent them off. The VP shook their paws and bade them a goodnight. Jill and Harvey excused themselves. "Early day tomorrow." Jill would take up tour duty and Harvey would once more be working at throwing hardware into the sky. Grigor stayed on.

The remaining Octavians closed ranks around the table and the Gaean contingent leaned in to be part of the discussion.

The Great Bear cleared his throat with a portentous rumble. "Our subject is exoplanet Rhea. Can I assume all of you are familiar with that world in Alpha Centauri?"

Affirmative nods.

"Rhea until recently was, in spite of its governmental structure, actually controlled by a revolutionary cabal headed up by a Zebra named Admiral Tumult. He had a mad scheme for cosmic conquest, claiming Rhea needed additional living space. Gaea and Earth were two of his targets. The good news is he is now dead."

Smiles.

"The bad news is that his plot is still being pursued by the Council's Chief Executive, his niece and members of their military."

Frowns and coughs.

"What you may not know is, for reasons we can't determine, the denizens of Rhea are incapable of the unassisted Quantum travel that you and we enjoy. Or at least most of us. *(A glance in Grigor's direction)* None of them are Adepts. To carry out their invasions, they acquired large scale Multiverse Transit hardware and software but were unable to make it work. In violation of all interplanetary and intergalactic agreements, we intervened and permanently destroyed their systems."

Sighs of relief.

"However, we do not believe they will be permanently forestalled. And I wonder about Woodrow Wolverine's recent defection to Rhea. Madam Vice President. We have done our part. With the consent of you and your party, I am turning over the responsibility to deal with the Rhean threat as you see fit. You are an immediate target. We will cut off their ability to replace their technology but as we say on Earth, the ball is now in your court."

The Lioness looked around at the assembled body. "Well, Doctor Bear, you certainly know how to show someone a good time. A bitter end to a pleasant evening. However, thank you for your assistance and information. I think we'll agree to accept your challenge although exactly what we'll do and how we'll do it will be up to a much more diverse group than this party here tonight. The President and other key members of the legislature must be informed. The military, our technologists and diplomats will give us advice and counsel. But this must be dealt with."

"I agree with your concern about the Wolverine. He will be recalled, voluntarily or otherwise. We'll let you know of our plans to the extent security allows. Meanwhile, I hope you and your group enjoy your stay with us. Grigor has been known to throw excellent parties. I wish you a good evening "

She rose, shook paws with Belinda and Octavius, nodded to the rest of the Octavians, beckoned her security detail and with her governmental entourage, who had remained silent throughout the discussion, briskly left the room.

Grigor, with eyebrows raised, got up and bowed. "I'll see you in the morning. Jill has a busy schedule planned for all of you, especially the Twins."

Momentary silence descended on the team. Howard shook his head partly in sorrow about Priscilla, partly in dismay at the situation. It was up to Otto, as usual to break the ice. He gave a goofy grin and said, "I sure hope that volcano enjoyed the meal I sent."

Laughs all around as the group, led by Belinda, left the room in search of a nightcap. She poked Octavius. "Thank you for detaching. I was afraid we were about to get into another scrape."

He stared at her. "Not this time, my love! Let's just enjoy the trip."

Epilogue

The lounge is packed full with her friends.
And Giselle's Tarot act just transcends.
With Sir Otto's assist,
She's too good to resist
And this is where our story ends.

The Polar Paradise Show Lounge was sold out in anticipation of the new act opening this evening – Madame Giselle, Queen of the Tarot and Otto The Magnificent. Mystery! Magic! and Madcap Mirth!

The Octavians had returned from their enjoyable Multiverse Tour at Gaea and along with L. Condor, Byzz and Huntley had all shuttled from the Bear's Lair to Abeardeen Airport and the Shetlands to cheer the performers on. Chita had been at the castle helping to work out the kinks, enhance the show biz values and develop the chatter and patter of the new act. Ursula 14 had worked out an Augmented Reality routine with Giselle, doing instant searches on her Tarot clients so Giselle could make 'amazing' comments and predictions. Dougal and Ms. Fairbearn had spared no efforts in creating an aura of mystery in the Show Lounge lighting, décor and sound effects. The house band had worked up a series of musical intros and stings to support Otto's and Giselle's spectacular feats.

The Great Bear, Belinda, Maury and the Twins occupied front row seats. The Frau, Wyatt, Howard, Chita, Condo, Byzz, Huntley and the Flying Tigers were also front and center around them. Even Marlin had flown over in his tank. While he was at the castle, he planned to visit his former boss, the Prince of Whales with Harold the Otter's help. Bruce Wallaroo, Tilda, Agent Honey Badger and Jack the Lad couldn't make it but sent best wishes. Lord David and Dancing Dan sat with Lion and Unicorn while Fiona, the four sheep waitresses and Mrs. McRadish were offering drinks and snacks to the large audience of Polar tourists. A packed theater.

Promptly at eight, the house lights dimmed and a drum roll grew in volume and speed. Otto "zapped' onstage from nowhere and executed a series of backflips ending in a kneeling bow with arms spread as the brass exploded with an exciting fanfare. Ta-Da! Wild applause. "How did he do that? Where did he come from?" The Octavians knew, The tourists didn't.

"Ladies and Gentlebeasts," he shouted, "Welcome to the Polar Paradise Show Lounge. I am obviously not Madame Giselle. *(Laughter)* As you've probably concluded, I am Hairy Otter, known in some circles as Otto the Magnificent. We're delighted you've chosen to join us this evening where we are prepared to awe you and entertain you."

He bowed again and straightened his red satin jacket. "Now, let me introduce the mysterious mistress of cartomancy, Madame Giselle, Queen of the Tarot."

The band played an exotic oriental melody as Giselle made her entrance, bathed in a spotlight. Clad in a sparkling gold lamé robe with a small matching turban perched between her ears, she bowed to the audience's enthusiastic applause, nodded to Otto and proceeded to the elaborately decorated table and chairs positioned in the center of the stage. Once she was seated, Otto looked at her and asked, "Madame, are the spirits active tonight?"

"Mais Oui, Monsieur Otto. They are quite eager to help our friends reach new wisdom."

"Well, let's begin!"

"Will you fetch the cards for me please?"

Suddenly a cascade of cards *(under Otto's telekinetic control)* tumbled out of the air and landed in a neat stack in front of the Bichon. (Ooohs and aaahs from the audience.)

She barked, "Very clever, Mon Ami. Shall I do a quick reading for you?"

"Of course, make a prediction."

"First you must cut and shuffle the cards."

The deck rose from the table, broke into two halves, shuffled itself and settled back on the surface, face down. *(Amazed laughter)*

He chortled, "There! So much easier to let them do it themselves. You know what a klutz I am."

"Indeed, let me take a moment to explain the Tarot deck for those in the audience who are not familiar with it." She gave a short tutorial and then waved Otto into the other chair.

"You have just returned from several journeys, am I correct?"

"Unfortunately, yes!"

"Let us see if the cards have anything to say about that. As you know, the Tarot is also known as the Fool's Journey. I shall take 3 cards."

"Well, I'm certainly the Fool."

She flipped the top card. "Indeed, you are. Here is the Fool. Let us take the next card. Ah. The Chariot. Your journey begins. And now The third Card The Wheel of Fortune. Are you ready to embark and bring fortune with you?"

He disappeared. *(zapped)* Murmurs throughout the audience. Suddenly a squeaky voice resonated from the back of the room. "Here I am, Madame. Journey's end. I have your first seeker ready to join you. Come with me, Miss."

He led a slender Polar Sow up to the stage. "Madame Giselle. This is Ms. Phoebe Polara. She seeks your guidance."

"Thank you, Otto. Please be seated Ms. Polara. Have we ever met or do we have mutual acquaintances?"

"Er, No! I just arrived today. I just wandered in here to see the show. I don't know either of you."

"D'accord!" A message flashed across her contact lenses. Ursula 14 on the job. "She's a librarian on vacation, by herself and looking for romance."

"Am I correct that you are here alone?"

"Yes! I'm on vacation."

"Away from all those books and disrupting cubs."

127

"How did you know I'm a librarian?"

"The spirits informed me. Now let us see what is in store for you."

She handed the deck to the sow who clumsily cut and shuffled the cards and gave them back.

Giselle peeled off and laid out three cards. She turned them over slowly and said, "I see an important change in your life. A pleasant change. You will find romance soon."

Phoebe gasped, clasped Giselle's paw and stepped back on the stage. Otto was on the side of the room with a large Polar male in tow. Ursula flashed on Giselle's contact lenses. "Single, rich, stockbroker, former military, socially unskilled."

"Bon Soir, Monsieur or should I call you Major?"

He reacted in amazement. "That was quite a while back and actually I was a Lieutenant Colonel"

"Je m'excuse de mon erreur. It was a late promotion?"

"Actually, Yes.

"What can the spirits help you with?"

"I don't know. I'd just like something new in my life."

"Perhaps, _someone_ new?"

"Well, yes!"

"Let us see!" She handed him the deck which he skillfully shuffled and then cut.

Otto chuckled. "Had some experience with cards, eh?"

"A bit." He placed the deck face down and Giselle picked off the top three cards.

"It seems you have attracted the ladies. The Queen of Wands, the Queen of Swords and the Empress. All good signs of a blossoming relationship."

Otto leaned over and said. "May I introduce you two. Colonel, meet Phoebe. Phoebe meet the Colonel." Laughter and applause as the two of them left the stage.

And so it went. Otto amazing the audience with his slapstick tricks, Giselle pretending annoyance at his antics and reading the Tarot cards for six or seven more clients.

Finally the band started to play Giselle's exit music. She rose and bowed. "Mesdames and Messieurs. Merci Beaucoup. My associate and I are so pleased that you have joined us this evening. I hope you feel the spirits made our little offering entertaining and valuable. Please join us again. We perform four nights a week and I can be reached by appointment as well. Thank you again. Au Revoir. Say goodnight, Otto!"

He sent the Tarot deck flying into the air, executed several back flips and caught the cards in a stack before they fell to th floor.

A standing ovation as the two of them took several bows while the band played their exit music. As the room started to empty, the Octavians ran up to the stage. Hugs and paw shakes. The Twins mobbed her. Octavius and Belinda were all smiles. Giselle was shaking with excitement and nervousness.

She turned to Chita. "Was it all right?"

The cat purred. "All right? Honey, you and your lutrine buddy were just sensational. Welcome back to show-biz."

THE END

THE OCTAVIAN CASES

BOOK 17

THE CASEBOOKS OF OCTAVIUS BEAR

About the Author

Harry DeMaio is a ***nom de plume*** of Harry B. DeMaio, successful author of several books on Information Security and Business Networks as well as the seventeen-volume ***Casebooks of Octavius Bear.*** He is also a published author for Belanger Books and the MX Sherlock Holmes series. A retired business executive, former consultant, information security specialist, elected official, private pilot, disk jockey and graduate school adjunct professor, he whiles away his time traveling and writing preposterous books, articles and stories.

He has appeared on many radio and TV shows and is an accomplished, frequent public speaker.

Former New York City natives, he and his extremely patient and helpful wife, Virginia, live in Cincinnati (and several other parallel universes.) They have two sons, Mark, living in Scottsdale, Arizona and Andrew. in Cortlandt Manor, New York, both of whom are quite successful and quite normal, thus putting the lie to the theory that insanity is hereditary.

His e-mail is hdemaio@zoomtown.com

You can also find him on Facebook.

His website is www.tavighostbooks.com

His books are available on Amazon, Barnes and Noble, and other fine bookstores as well as directly from MX Publishing and Belanger Books.